DM

CINDERELLA
AND THE
COWBOY

CINDERELLA AND THE COWBOY

BY

JUDY CHRISTENBERRY

MILLS & BOON®
Pure reading pleasure™

First published in Great Britain 2008
Large Print edition 2009
Harlequin Mills & Boon Limited,
Eton House, 18-24 Paradise Road,
Richmond, Surrey TW9 1SR

© Judy Russell Christenberry 2008

ISBN: 978 0 263 20583 1

Set in Times Roman 17½ on 22 pt.
16-0409-35323

Printed and bound in Great Britain
by CPI Antony Rowe, Chippenham, Wiltshire

CHAPTER ONE

ELIZABETH Ransom struggled off the bus, carefully leading her toddler son down the stairs while carrying her baby in a pouch across her chest.

"This is his driveway, ma'am," the gentlemanly bus driver said as he held out her luggage. "You can't miss the house. It's the only one on this road."

Finding the house wasn't the part she was worried about. It was what would happen when she got there. "Thank you for your help. You've been very kind."

"Mommy?"

She looked down at her three-year-old. "Yes, Brady?"

"Where is my grandpa?"

"Just a little farther and we'll meet him." As the bus pulled away, she looked around at the tall weeds growing alongside the drive. "First we're going to stow our luggage here where no one can see them." She put the two suitcases behind the weeds, hoping that her son wouldn't ask why. She didn't have the heart to tell him they might not be staying.

She said a private prayer that her father-in-law would at least offer hospitality for a few days. She prayed too that Tom Ransom had heard of his son's death; she didn't want to break the news that his son had recently been killed in a car accident.

Forcing a smile at her child, she took his hand. "Let's walk to Grandpa's house, okay, Brady?"

"Is it very far, Mommy?"

"I don't know, honey, but the bus driver said it was at the end of this road."

"I'm cold, Mommy."

Early December in Oklahoma could be a lot worse, she knew; still, there was a biting wind. "If we walk faster, we'll get warm." She led her son down the road. After a few minutes he noticeably tired. "Keep walking, sweetheart."

As they picked up the pace, she heard the baby awakening and soothed her with her voice. Poor Jenny. She would never know her daddy.

On second thought, perhaps that was for the best, seeing as how Reggie Ransom was far from a model father. He'd walked out on them one afternoon, and she hadn't seen him since. Only when she managed to reach him and remind him of their existence did he bother sending any money for rent and food.

She always knew Reggie wasn't the type to be tied down by a wife and kids. He wanted a carefree life, wining and dining on the rodeo circuit where he was a star.

But Elizabeth had wanted a family to belong to so badly that she ignored her intuition and married him anyway, right after college. Especially after she found herself pregnant. She remembered thinking she was going to have everything she'd ever wanted.

Too bad Reggie hadn't felt the same.

As soon as they were married he told her he had to go back on the circuit.

Elizabeth kept them afloat with her teaching job, paying the rent and Brady's day care bills. But when she got pregnant with Jenny and took ill, she couldn't work. Money was tight. Now Jenny was six weeks old, but with the school year started, Elizabeth had to wait for the next semester to be hired.

She needed help now.

Tom Ransom was her only hope. She hoped

her father-in-law could offer just a little to help them along.

"Mommy?" Brady grabbed her hand and tugged on it. "Mommy? Is that his house?"

She looked up, surprised to see a white clapboard house and several outbuildings in front of her. "Yes, I think so, Brady. It's very nice, isn't it?"

"Yeah!" After a moment Brady asked, "Do you think Grandpa will like me?"

"I'm sure he will. You look a lot like your daddy."

"Is that good?"

"Your daddy was a handsome man." She didn't mention her husband's deficits, his abandonment of his family, spending all the money he made on other women and booze. No child needed to hear that.

"Mommy, I see Grandpa! Can I go tell him it's us coming to visit?"

She shaded her eyes and looked up at a tall, rugged man standing by a pickup. "Honey, I don't think that's your grandpa. That man's too young. You'd better stay with me."

She refused to give credence to the fear that clawed at her throat. Had this man bought the land from her husband's father?

The man must have seen them, because he got in the pickup and drove down the drive to them.

"Are you coming to the ranch?"

The man looked to be in his early thirties, with dark-brown hair under a Stetson. A typical rancher, she thought. But was he an owner? "Yes, if...if it still belongs to Tom Ransom."

"It does."

Her sigh of relief was audible. "If you don't mind, we'd appreciate a ride to the house."

He nodded toward the passenger seat. "Get in."

She helped Brady climb into the truck and

then pulled herself and her baby up, feeling old beyond her years.

"I'm Elizabeth Ransom. I've come to visit my father-in-law."

"You're Reggie Ransom's wife?" There was shock in his voice.

"He told his father about us?" she asked, feeling pleased.

"No, ma'am. If Tom had known you'd existed, he'd have brought you out here a long time ago."

So much for her good feelings. "I...I hope he'll at least let us stay a few days."

The man only grunted.

He said nothing until they'd pulled up in front of the house. A large house, huge in comparison to the tiny one-bedroom apartment in which they'd lived.

"I'll come get you down," the man said gruffly. He hopped down and then came around to her door. "Hey, little guy, you want to come over here and let me help you down?"

"Okay," Brady said, climbing over his mother's knees. "Will you catch me?"

"Sure I will." When he took the boy to the porch, Brady looked at his mother.

In spite of her tiredness, Elizabeth scooted down off the high seat.

"I'll go tell Tom you're here." He turned back. "Just a minute. Where are your bags?"

"W-we left the bags in the grass by the front gate."

She followed him inside the back door, into the kitchen. Looking around the room, recently updated and spacious, she hungered for such a lovely working environment.

The man came back to the kitchen. "Tom's waiting."

"Thank you. Brady, let's go meet your

grandfather." She took the boy's hand as he moved closer to her.

She followed the man down a long hallway, realizing for the first time that she never got his name. He stopped at the last door and opened it.

Elizabeth stepped into a large bedroom, where a man sat in a wing back chair in front of a glowing fireplace. He looked to be in his sixties, with a receding hairline pushing back his graying brown hair.

"Mr. Ransom," she whispered. "I'm Elizabeth Ransom, your son's widow. This is my…our son, Brady, and our daughter, Jennifer."

"Come in, Elizabeth," he said in a small voice. "I'm glad to meet you."

"Thank you, sir. I'm pleased to meet you."

Tom shifted his gaze to the boy. "Brady? Come here, boy. You look like your daddy when he was your age."

"Really?"

"Yeah. And the little one?" he asked Elizabeth. "How old is she?"

"She was born six weeks ago."

"You doing all right? It's tough to make a trip when your baby is that young."

"Yes, she came a little early because of…of the news I received."

"Tom, I hate to interrupt but I need to go get their bags." She'd almost forgotten that the man she'd met out on the driveway was in the room. "They left them in the grass by the gate."

"Okay, Jack, thanks."

At least now she knew his name. Jack.

When the door closed behind him, she knew the time had come to make her plea.

"Mr. Ransom, I'm here because…" She ducked her head, unable to make eye contact. "Because I need help. I'll be able to get a teaching job for the next semester but…but I don't know how we'll make it until then. I wondered if the kids and I could stay here."

"But he was doing well, wasn't he?" There was such sadness in the man's voice.

"I don't know. He sent me money every once in a while, but not often."

"So he left you broke?"

She pressed her lips together and dug in her purse. "Here's my copy of our marriage certificate. Yes, he left me broke."

"I'm sorry." Did she detect a note of anger in his tone? "I know he made a lot of money. He shouldn't have left you broke."

"I can get a job when the new semester starts, sir. It won't be forever that we'll hang on to your sleeve. I promise—"

Tom held up a hand. "Don't worry about it. I've got lots of room here. Stay as long as you want."

Elizabeth blinked away the tears. "Thank

you. I can keep the kitchen clean and do the housework while we're here."

"We usually have a lady come in to clean once a week."

"Who does your cooking?"

"Me and Jack just manage. We take turns, and sometimes we eat in the bunkhouse."

"I don't want to intrude, but I could cook for you."

"Don't feel you have to."

She smiled. "I'd be pleased to cook for you, Mr. Ransom."

"Let's make it first names, Elizabeth."

"Thank you, Tom."

He stood up and held out his hand. "Welcome home."

Jack Crawford revved the engine of the pickup as he wended down the driveway from the house. He'd seen the look on Tom's face when he laid eyes on his grandson. His old friend had been hooked like a fish at sunrise.

He shut the engine at the gate and got out to search for the woman's bags. Why would she hide them in the weeds? Probably so she wouldn't look too needy when she came to the door.

Instead she stood there, looking maternal, holding her son's hand and her daughter against her chest. The firelight had cast highlights on her light-brown hair and illuminated her tall, thin frame.

Not that Tom would notice those things about her. He'd been too focused on the kids.

His grandkids.

Jack knew Tom Ransom too well. Beneath that crusty cowboy exterior beat the heart of the most righteous, kind and honorable man he knew.

Tom would do the right thing.

Starting today, the Ransom Ranch would have three new boarders.

Maybe the kids were just what Tom needed to come out of the funk he'd fallen into since his wife's death and his son's departure. He'd lost interest in the ranch years ago, then lost interest in most everything. If it hadn't been for Jack, he would've sold the ranch long ago. Jack had been making it viable, turning a profit on the 2500-acre cattle ranch, and keeping Tom going at the same time.

But now…?

No, Jack couldn't blame Tom. The woman and her kids were family, after all.

But where did that leave him?

"I've got your bags. Where do they go?"

Elizabeth started at the sound of Jack's deep voice behind her. She turned from the cabinets where she was checking out the cooking supplies. "I don't know. I didn't ask Tom."

He started for the hallway. "Come on. I'll find places for you. He needs to get some rest."

She gave him a troubled stare, then followed him. Beside her, Brady picked up the diaper bag. "I can carry this one, Mommy."

"That's wonderful of you, Brady. Your sister will be glad to have her bag with us." She followed Jack up the stairs. "Tom said we could live here for a while," she told him.

"Yeah, I thought he would."

"I offered to cook for the two of you. He said you took turns and sometimes ate in the bunkhouse. Which would you prefer?"

He swung around and gave her a studied look. He didn't exude the warmth she'd found in Tom.

"It depends. How well do you cook?"

She straightened. "I've been told I'm good."

Jack's eyes swept her, as if sizing her up. Before he could reply, Brady spoke up. "Mommy's pancakes are really good!"

"Is that so?" he asked, never taking his eyes off Elizabeth.

"Yeah, they're yummy. Baby doesn't eat them, but Mommy makes them for me."

"That's good enough for me. I'm up for pancakes."

"But we don't eat pancakes for dinner, Brady," Elizabeth reminded her boy, grateful for the diversion.

"What do we have for dinner, Mommy?"

"I don't know, sweetie. I'll have to see what they have."

"Trust me," Jack said. "We have everything you need."

There was something in the way he said it that made her think he wasn't talking about food. She cleared her throat and changed the subject. "What room shall we take?"

"Well, I think Brady should take the room on this side. It's next to mine. And you should take the room on this side of the stairs, and put the little one next to you."

"We don't need that many rooms. We can share one."

"I believe Tom would like you to each have your own room. He wants you comfortable."

"I don't—"

Jack apparently wasn't entertaining her excuses. "Come to your new room, Brady. Bring your suitcase with you. I'll help you unpack."

"No! I'll unpack for him."

"You've got to unpack for yourself and the baby."

"I'll manage."

"In that case, then, can I take Brady to the

barn so he can see some puppies that were born a couple of weeks ago?"

"Please, Mommy?" Brady pleaded with his mother.

"Yes, if you'll do what Jack says."

"Okay, Mommy!" Brady hugged her legs and then held his hand up for Jack.

Jack took it. "We'll be back for dinner."

Elizabeth stood there, watching her little boy walk off with Jack. The unfamiliar sight of Brady with a man nearly brought tears to her eyes. How she'd yearned over the years for Reggie to be there for him, to be a real daddy.

Casting off the regret, she took the larger bag into the bedroom Jack had suggested she take. The large room was half the size of their entire apartment, with more storage than she needed for the clothes she owned.

In Jenny's room she found a twin bed but no

crib. She could put Jenny to bed there with pillows all around. For the time being, she figured. She wouldn't grow enough to need a baby bed until they moved on.

She sighed. She had so much to do to bring her children up right. When Reggie was killed, she shouldn't have been relieved, but she'd already known their marriage was a mistake. He hadn't cared about her, not when he moved on to the next available woman. He'd never touched her after she got pregnant with Jenny.

She remembered that night. He'd come home drunk and had taken her to the bedroom and had sex with her. The next morning he didn't remember anything he'd done. Then he'd claimed she'd betrayed him when she turned up pregnant.

The only reason she'd stayed with him was that she wanted her son to have what she never had. She shivered at the memory.

She'd been five when she'd been taken away from her mother by Child Services, never to be returned. The emotions of that day flooded her again, swamping her with sadness and fear. She'd never known her father.

More than anything, she wanted her children to have family, someone who would always help, offer comfort. She'd have to be their family now. Because of Reggie she didn't think she'd ever remarry.

After hugging her little girl and promising her a future, she put Jenny on the bed and surrounded her with pillows. Then she stowed the child's belongings.

She went to the kitchen after unpacking for Brady and surveyed the full pantry and freezer, packed with any cut of beef she wanted to cook. The refrigerator was her final review. Jack was right. They had anything she'd need to cook dinner tonight.

Half an hour later, Brady ran into the room. "Mommy! They have lots of puppies. They don't have their eyes open yet. And they wiggle a lot!"

"I'm glad, Brady. Now you need to hang up your coat and go wash your hands so you'll be ready for dinner."

"But, Mommy, can I have a puppy?"

Elizabeth whirled around and stared at her son. "What did you say?"

"Jack said I could have one."

She turned and stared at Jack. "You told him what?"

"I suggested he could pick out a dog if you didn't mind."

"No! No, he can't have a puppy! Brady, go wash up."

"But, Mommy—"

"Go, Brady!"

The little boy went into the bathroom on the bottom floor. Elizabeth knew his heart was broken, but she had no choice.

"Why can't the boy have a dog?"

Not that it was any of his business, she thought, but she told him anyway. "Because I can't take a dog with us when we leave."

"You sure Tom is going to let you leave?"

Elizabeth looked at him then. What did he mean by that? And did she detect a note of sarcasm in Jack's tone? Somehow, she didn't think he was in favor of them being there.

Until she got the lay of the land, she thought it best to simply avoid the subject with Jack. Instead she asked him to get Tom to the table for dinner. He merely gave her a nod and walked out of the room.

She'd made a beef and cheese macaroni meal with a salad and hot rolls. It wasn't elegant, but it was quick, hot and filling.

Just as she put it on the table, Tom came in, holding on to Jack's arm.

She smiled warmly at the older man. "Good evening, Tom."

"Are you all moved in already?" Tom asked as he sat down.

"Yes, we are, in very spacious quarters."

"Good, good. You're family. And I'm thrilled to have you and the kids here. Where's the baby?"

"She's napping. She'll be up for a bottle at eight, after dinner."

"It occurred to me that we'll need to get a crib. Jack can go with you to buy one and whatever else you need."

She shook her head. "I can't afford to buy anything right now. We're all right. I have her surrounded by pillows."

"Nonsense, Elizabeth. I'll pay for the crib and other things you need. My son did a poor job of taking care of you and your babies. It's my job now. I'll provide for you. You and Jack can shop tomorrow."

She fought to hold back her tears, blinking rapidly. "Tom, I really appreciate your offer, but we won't be able to take much with us when we leave, so there's no reason to buy them."

Tom frowned. "Honey, I'm not planning on you leaving. Like I said, you're family. The only family I have left. Jack, here, has been like a son to me since Reggie went away. I was too easy on my son. I didn't make him learn good and bad. I wondered why God took him and not me. Now I know I still have purpose here on earth. I have you, Brady and little Jenny. God left me here to do what my son should've done."

She gave up the fight and let the tears fall. "Tom, I promise I didn't come here for you to take care of us. I can get a job when school starts again."

"Do you like teaching school?"

"It's not bad."

"Wouldn't you rather raise your kids?"

"Yes, but—"

"How about cooking?"

"I enjoy cooking, and will be glad to cook for you and Jack, Tom. That…that would be like having a family."

"That's what we want, too." Tom leaned forward and patted her hand. "You just take care of the house and those kids and let us know if you need anything, okay?" Before she could reply he continued, "And while you're at the store, me and Brady can get to know each other."

She swiped at her tears. "I don't know what to say, Tom. Thank you."

"You're welcome. Now, no more tears,

young lady. We're going to wear happy faces around here from now on."

Elizabeth couldn't help but smile.

Her smile lasted through dinner and the cleanup. Jack insisted on helping, despite her protests, and she thought maybe she'd won him over.

"What time's breakfast in the morning?" he asked as they finished up.

"Brady usually gets up about seven. Is that okay?"

"Fine. And after breakfast, you and I will drive into Oklahoma City to do some shopping."

"We don't have to, Jack. I don't think Tom will even notice if we don't buy much."

Jack shot her a look that wiped away her smile. "I may be Tom's friend, Elizabeth, but I'm also his employee. I do what I'm told to do."

CHAPTER TWO

ELIZABETH didn't accept Jack's warning. When she got up the next morning, she fully intended to blow off the shopping trip.

She hurriedly dressed and slipped downstairs to make breakfast. Pancakes were bubbling on the griddle when she heard steps on the stairway. From the sound, she figured it was Jack coming down the stairs. But she was surprised when he appeared with Brady in his arms.

"Brady, did you forget to get dressed?"

The little boy giggled. "Jack said I could come down in my pajamas."

"I see."

"It's okay, isn't it?"

She ignored Jack's question and smiled at her son. "Hop up in your seat, sweetie."

"Okay, Mommy," Brady said.

She flipped the pancakes onto plates and brought them to the table, already set with butter and syrup.

"These look good, Elizabeth," Jack said.

She didn't respond, choosing to pour milk for Brady instead.

"I'd like some milk, too, please," Jack said.

She poured another glass.

As she turned back to the stove to flip the four new pancakes, Tom's door opened and the man came to the table.

He looked better than yesterday. Sprier, brighter. "Good morning, Tom. How are you this morning?"

Jack greeted Tom also.

Brady grinned at his grandfather. "Good morning, Grandpa!"

"Brady, that's the best greeting I've heard in a long time."

"Mommy made pancakes for us."

"I can see that."

Just then Elizabeth put a plate down in front of him.

They all ate in silence. Elizabeth didn't get upset that they didn't rave about her pancakes. She knew they were good.

When breakfast was over, she sent Brady up to his room to get dressed. Tom went back to his bedroom when he finished.

Jack got up and filled a cup with coffee and sat back down again.

"Do you want more pancakes?"

He looked up in surprise. "No, I'm full. But they were wonderful."

"Thank you."

She continued to do the dishes. After a few minutes Jack said, "I can finish the dishes. Why don't you go ahead and get ready so we can get on our way."

"I'm not going anywhere."

"Look, Elizabeth, I told you last night. I've got my orders and I intend to follow them. Whether or not you agree."

Elizabeth turned and gave him an icy stare. "What are you going to do? Carry me out against my will?"

"If I have to."

His stare was just as frigid as she maintained an even eye contact.

Seconds passed before an idea struck Elizabeth. She'd go with him and make him think he was taking Tom's orders, but she wouldn't buy anything.

Wiping her hands on the dish towel she

held, she never broke eye contact when she said, "I'll be ready in two minutes."

Then she walked out of the kitchen without another word.

Jack chuckled under his breath as Elizabeth walked out of the room. She'd had such a full head of steam, he figured she wasn't backing down. He wondered what she had up her sleeve.

Regardless, he intended to follow Tom's orders to the letter.

When he heard her coming down the stairs, he jumped to his feet, only to find the two children with her.

"I need to take Brady to Tom's room."

He waited at the door as she gave the boy final instructions to not bother his grandfather.

"He'll be fine, Elizabeth. A little bothering never hurt no one."

She leaned down and kissed her son goodbye.

Then she walked out of the house, assuming Jack would follow.

He did.

Jack suggested they start with the infant department. He knew she intended to end it there, too, but that wouldn't be happening. Not on his watch.

As they looked at all the cribs they had on the floor, Jack noticed she paid more attention to the prices than the crib. But he saw the sparkle in her big blue eyes when she approached one in particular. Then he stepped to the saleslady and told her they would take the one she'd lingered over.

Elizabeth whirled around. "What did you just do?"

"I chose a crib."

"Why didn't I get to choose?"

"You did. I saw the way you were looking at that one."

"But—"

He ignored her and turned back to the saleslady. "We'll take it."

Elizabeth huffed.

"What else can I get you today?" the saleslady asked.

Elizabeth answered for him. "Nothing else. This will be all."

"I believe the lady asked me the question, Liz." He gave the older woman his full attention. "What would you recommend?"

She offered some suggestions, including bedding and a musical animal mobile for over the bed, pads for over the sheets, and springs to replace the rollers on the bed.

"I'll take it."

"All of them?" the saleslady asked Jack.

"Yeah, all of them."

Elizabeth glared at Jack. She knew what he was up to. "I will not participate in this!"

"That's fine. Why don't you go on to the boy's department and pick out Brady's clothes?"

"He doesn't need any clothes."

"We'll see."

Instead she sat down in the comfortable chair they had for customers and took Jenny out of the pouch across her chest. When the baby started to fuss, she gave her a bottle, all the time ignoring what that difficult man was doing.

Jack was having the time of his life. When he and the saleslady had rounded up everything, he asked what else they would need.

"Won't your wife want to help?"

He didn't bother correcting the woman. "No, she doesn't care. Let's pick out some pretty clothes for Jenny."

"But won't your wife be mad at you?"

"That makes making up a lot more fun," he said with a wink.

She gave a girlish giggle and went to work again. In no time she had a pile of pink in front of him.

"Okay, I think we've finished," Jack said. "You'll have them sent to Pickup for us, won't you?"

"Yes, of course. It's been a real pleasure, sir. I wish you and your wife all the happiness in the world."

"Thank you." He bent down and kissed her on the cheek.

"Are you finished now?" Elizabeth asked him as he approached her. "Jenny wants to go home."

Jack chuckled. "I suppose she told you that?"

"Yes."

"You're a terrible liar."

"I am not!"

He just grinned at her and said, "Ask Jenny what she wants to do."

Elizabeth pouted. "You needn't make fun of me."

"Right. Let's go."

When they reached the door to leave the store, he suddenly stopped. "Oh, Liz, I need to go to another area to get something for Brady. Tom asked me to pick out something special for him."

She frowned, but she couldn't say no to a special gift from a grandpa. "All right. And I should tell you that I don't like to be called Liz."

"Yes, ma'am." He tipped an imaginary hat. "What size does Brady wear?"

"Size six."

"Ah, I thought he was big for his age."

"Yes, he… What are you buying?"

"Why don't you find a seat for you and Jenny?"

"You won't be long, will you?"

"As long as it takes to find what I'm looking for."

"But—" She cut off when Jack walked away. Arguing was useless.

She sat back and watched him wander around the boy's department. He wouldn't be too long, she was sure.

But she was curious when he gathered a saleslady to follow him around. She gave an exasperated sigh.

After about half an hour, he finally returned.

"We have only one more stop," he said as he pulled Elizabeth toward the adjacent department.

When she saw the ladies' clothes she pulled up short. "No. We have nothing to buy here!"

"Yes, we do. If it's important for Tom to take you to church, then you should accommodate him. That's all I'm asking. Pick out a dress for church."

She finally agreed. Checking the prices, she went to the sales rack. As she did so, Jack unfastened the halter that she'd used to carry Jenny around.

"What are you doing?" she gasped as she felt her halter come undone.

"I'm making it easier for you. You'll have to try on the clothes."

"But—"

"Yes, I can handle little Jenny by myself."

Against her better judgment she picked out five dresses and let the saleslady take her to a dressing room.

"Oh, there are some clothes already in this dressing room," Elizabeth pointed out.

"Yes, your husband chose those dresses. He said you were to come show him all the clothes."

She shut the door gently, resisting the urge to slam it. Jack could try whatever he wanted, but he wouldn't get his way.

Jack grinned when the saleslady told him she didn't think his wife would be coming out. "Good. We need to get started."

With the woman's help, he chose an array of clothes and shoes.

About that time, Elizabeth came out of the dressing room carrying her choices. Jack met her. "You didn't come out and show me any of the outfits."

"No, I didn't."

"You didn't choose any of the outfits I picked out."

"No, I didn't like them."

He looked at her with narrowed eyes. "You didn't even try them on, did you? That's okay. We'll buy them anyway."

"No! I'll…I'll go try them on."

"And come out and show me?"

"Yes, I'll come out and show you." She said that with her teeth gritted.

"Good. Jenny and I will wait for you to appear."

He sat down in the chair and waited. Once she went in the dressing room, he handed his card to the saleslady. She charged all the things he'd bought and placed it all in closed bags to be sent to Pickup.

In the meantime, Elizabeth had come out in several of the dresses. Jack knew he'd gotten her size and coloring right; she looked beautiful in all of them.

When she finished all the outfits he'd chosen, she came out with her coat on. "Happy now?" she asked him.

"You didn't like any of them?"

"I don't need any of them," she replied, taking Jenny from him and putting on the harness. "Let's go get the dress I chose and go."

Jack shook his head. "I'll go pay for the dress but we're not going home yet. We've got to have lunch first. I'm starving."

"But—"

"Jenny's hungry." He flashed her a pearly white grin. "She told me."

He got his way, of course.

Elizabeth groaned as she realized he'd gotten his way the entire day. Starting from pancakes at breakfast to shopping to lunch.

She was never so grateful as when they got in his truck later that afternoon.

"Just stay here," Jack told her when they pulled up to the loading dock in the rear of the store. "I'll get them to put everything in the back."

Everything?

All she bought was one dress and a crib, plus the special gift he'd picked out for Tom to give Brady. How long could that take?

As she waited what seemed like a half hour, Jenny fell asleep. Her own eyes felt heavy and she closed them.

Jack went into the shipping room. He waited until he was sure Elizabeth had fallen asleep, then he asked for help in loading his purchases. He cautioned the men not to make noise.

His ruse was successful.

He was smiling when he eased the pickup out of the parking lot.

Once he was on the road, Elizabeth stirred. "Why didn't you wake me?" she asked, looking around.

"No need. Everything's taken care of." Jack had to wipe away the smile on the face.

She prepared a bottle for Jenny and had it

ready when the baby woke a few miles from the ranch.

As soon as he put the truck in Park, Jack came around and helped her out. "I'll bring the purchases up later."

"All right. I…I should say thank you."

"No need," he said with a shrug. "It was my pleasure."

Pleasure, indeed.

Once Jenny had eaten and fallen asleep, Jack suggested that Brady show his mom the puppies in the barn. She hesitated, then agreed once Brady had told her how much he missed her when she was gone.

As soon as they left, Jack figured he had a half hour to get things in place. He started with Brady's purchases, removing tags and putting things in the dresser and closet. Then he went to Elizabeth's room. The new underwear and clothes filled three drawers, and her closet took all the dresses on hangers and the shoes and high heels in neatly stacked boxes.

He had fifteen minutes left to fill Jenny's room. After putting away her shoes and coats he set up the baby monitor and mounded disposable diapers beside the bed. Then he ran downstairs and put the bed sheets and clothes in the wash as the saleslady had suggested.

Grabbing his tool set on the way back up, he started setting up the crib. That's where Elizabeth and Brady found him when they came in.

"What did my grandpa get me from town, Jack?" Brady whispered.

Jack replied in a matching tone. "It's hanging in the closet."

Elizabeth followed Brady as he bolted to his room.

She was back in a few minutes, a scowl on her face.

"Why did you buy him a sport coat and dress slacks?" She lowered her voice the moment she remembered her sleeping baby.

"Tom wanted Brady to be able to go to church with him."

"But I don't think that was necessary."

Jack merely shrugged his shoulders and went back to the crib setup.

"What else did you buy?" Elizabeth mused aloud as she began to look around the room. She was fuming. Here she thought she'd managed to pull one over on Jack, and instead he'd been the sly fox. But when she noticed the baby monitor on the dresser, she couldn't stop the smile.

Jack must have seen her face soften because he said, "I thought you might enjoy the diapers even more."

"You bought diapers?"

He nodded to the bedside and the closet.

She found two boxes of larger-size ones in the closest. On the trip she'd used disposable diapers but they were about to run out. Without cash she figured she'd have to resort to cotton ones again. But not now.

Thanks to Tom. And Jack.

She turned to him and said thanks.

He grinned at her. "Glad to hear that I did something good."

"I didn't mean you—" Chastised, she hung her head. "I'm sorry. I wasn't very nice about shopping today, but you were good to me."

"Um, don't praise me too much," he muttered.

"Why not? You bought some things that Jenny needs."

"I hope so." After a minute he said, "You'd better go put the wash in the dryer."

"What wash?"

"Jenny's sheets and blankets." He hesitated, then added, "And a few other things."

She didn't bother asking for an explanation. Running down the stairs, she went to the laundry room to see what was going on. When she opened the washing machine, she found a barrelful of outfits, blankets, sheets. She put all the laundry into the dryer and went back upstairs.

"You did an interesting job of shopping, didn't you?"

He looked up at her standing in the doorway. "Yeah, the saleslady was really good."

"Yes, I see she really earned her commission. Though I'm not sure Jenny will be little long enough to wear all of this."

"Tom wanted the best."

"Yes, I guess so."

After a moment she asked, "Did you put my dress in my room?"

"Um, yeah, I did, but could you help me with this last piece? I need another pair of hands to finish this crib."

She knelt down beside him and held the bar sides while he worked them into the ends. This close to him, she noticed his muscular forearms and strong hands. Against her better judgment she let her eyes travel up his arms to his neck and face. Was he wearing cologne on his neck, or was that woodsy scent his own? It seemed to suit him. She could easily picture him out on his horse, swinging his Stetson as he rounded up cattle.

He turned to her then, and she was struck by the blueness of his eyes. Was this the first time she noticed their color? A blue so unlike her own, more like the sky on a clear Oklahoma day.

"Okay, now we have to stand the crib up."

His voice broke into her daydream, and she hurried to her feet to follow his order.

When they had the crib upright, Jack pushed it and watched it rock gently. "Another suggestion from the saleslady."

She nodded in approval. "That's nice, Jack. Thank you."

"You're welcome, Elizabeth."

Their eyes lingered on each other a little too long, and she suddenly felt uncomfortable. "I…I'm going to check on my dress," she said as she went to the door.

"Uh, Elizabeth, you might… Don't be mad at me, okay?"

She stopped. "Why do you think—" Standing akimbo, she assumed a menacing tone. "Jack Crawford, what did you do?"

He shrugged. "It's just a few extra things."

She ran for her room.

Jack went downstairs, as if in search of cover.

Brady caught up to him after coming out of Tom's room. "Thank you, Jack."

"For what, Brady?"

"Grandpa said you picked out all those clothes for me."

"Now you have extra things so your mom won't have to do so much laundry." He hunkered low so that his eyes were level with the boy. "Do me a favor, Brady, and let's not tell your mom just yet."

That's when they heard Elizabeth scream.

CHAPTER THREE

JACK didn't move fast enough. Before he could exit the kitchen, Elizabeth appeared in front of him, enraged.

"Jack, how could you do this! I don't need all those clothes! And six dresses! That's ridiculous!"

He affected a calmness he didn't feel. "Now, Elizabeth, you don't know how many dresses you'll need here. Tom is well liked."

"I don't care how well liked he is. That's not the point. You tricked me. And made a fool of me." Her eyes flashed fire. "I don't appreciate that."

He speared her with a look. "Like you weren't planning to trick me?"

"Hey, y'all. What's all the yelling about?" Tom asked as he came into the kitchen.

Jack read the expression on Elizabeth's face and knew she didn't want Tom to know what she'd tried to do. Because he feared it would hurt Tom, he went along.

"Sorry, Tom. Elizabeth felt like I spent too much on her and the kids, that's all."

"But you told me what you spent. I didn't feel it was excessive," Tom said calmly.

"But, Tom, I couldn't possibly need six dresses."

"That's not the point. We just want you to be happy, Elizabeth. And I can afford it, so why not let me provide for you. After all, my son didn't provide for his family."

Elizabeth smiled at him. "Well, you certainly have taken care of that, Tom. And Jack certainly did a good job."

The older man grinned at his longtime friend. "He always has, Elizabeth. I knew he'd do what I asked him to do."

"There was one thing I forgot, Tom," Jack interjected. "A new coat for Elizabeth."

"I have a winter coat already. I was wearing it when we arrived."

As if she hadn't spoken, Tom agreed with Jack. "Good. We'll plan on you going again."

Elizabeth stood there with her mouth open, and Jack couldn't stop the big smile from overtaking his face.

"I don't know about you, but I need to get started on supper." Elizabeth began pulling ingredients out of the refrigerator, grateful for the diversion. How could Jack simply ignore her like that? Tom was well meaning, she knew, but Jack could have been the voice of reason. Instead he added fuel to the fire.

"What are we having?" Jack asked, coming up beside her.

"A Mexican dish."

"Is that all you're going to tell me?"

"I don't think you need to know much more. Don't you trust me?" She gave him a saccharine look.

"Not with that chili sauce in your hand." He nodded toward the bottle she held. "I'm afraid my constitution isn't made to withstand too much heat."

"Then you needn't worry." She got out a thick cutting board to chop onions and chili peppers.

She nearly laughed at his expression when he saw the chilis.

"Uh, maybe I'd better go put a clean sheet on the crib and transfer Jenny to her very own bed."

"Thanks, Jack. And bring the monitor down, will you?"

When he left the room, Elizabeth picked up

another chili. She hefted it in her hand and debated silently. Should she?

Dinner was ready when Tom and Brady came in from playing with the puppies in the barn and Jack finished up some ranch chores.

She admonished them all to wash up before taking their seats at the table.

"If you'll pass your plates, I'll serve the casscrole." She noticed Jack didn't budge and stifled a laugh. "You go first, Brady. Grandpa and Jack will try it after you."

Brady held his plate up to his mother. She gave him a spoonful of the casserole. Then she filled Tom's plate with two spoonfuls. When Jack finally offcred his plate, Elizabeth heaped on three servings.

"That's enough, Elizabeth. I'm not that hungry tonight."

"Nonsense," she said as she scooped out a

fourth spoonful. "I've seen you eat, remember?"

Jack hesitated, then finally took a bite. Then, as if surprised, he broke into a smile. "Delightful!"

"Not too hot for you, Jack?" she asked as innocently as a lamb.

"No, it's perfect, Elizabeth."

She returned his smile. "I told you you could trust me." But boy, she admitted to herself, how she'd been tempted!

Elizabeth heard Jenny stirring in her bed, making cooing sounds as she woke up.

Running up the stairs, she got there before the baby had a chance to really come awake. The others heard her tender words to baby Jenny.

Tom nodded. "She's a good mother. Just as I knew she'd be."

"Yeah, she's a good mommy." Brady grinned at his grandpa.

"I think we should do the dishes for her while she takes care of Jenny."

Brady jumped to his feet and in no time the three of them had the table cleared. They were loading the dishwasher when Elizabeth came down with Jenny.

"Why, thank you, guys. You did a great job."

"I helped, Mommy!"

"Of course you did, sweetie. You're a very good big boy."

"How's little Jenny?" Jack asked.

"Hungry."

"Here, I'll heat her bottle," Jack said.

"Thanks, Jack." She took a seat at the table and talked to Jenny. Brady pressed against his mother.

"Can she talk yet?" Brady asked.

"Not yet. But she can make sounds."

"Show me."

"Okay, Jenny, will you talk for your big brother? Come on, Jenny, say ooh."

The baby made ooh's for her mother.

Brady laughed and clapped, startling his sister with the loud noise. She burst into sobs, and he looked as if he was about to follow her. "Sorry, Mommy."

She bent down to kiss her son's cheek. "It's okay, Brady. Next time you'll know not to make any sudden noises."

He smiled up at her.

Jack brought the bottle to Elizabeth. "I checked it. It's just right."

"Thanks."

He smiled down at the baby. "Hi, there, Jenny."

She oohed for Jack, too.

"That's my girl," he said with a grin.

"Don't listen, Jenny," Elizabeth crooned to her daughter. "I bet he says that to all the girls."

She fed the baby her bottle, talking to her while she sucked the milk.

Tom and Jack sat down at the table, watching.

"I haven't even held my granddaughter yet," Tom said. "Do you...do you think I could feed her?"

"Sure, Tom." Elizabeth got up immediately and settled the baby in her grandfather's arms. "You're like a pro already," she noted with a pat on his shoulder as she hovered over him.

In the few days that they'd been here Elizabeth had seen a big change in Tom. He no longer spent most of the day in his room, either in bed or in his chair by the fire, choosing instead to spend time with Brady out in the barn or in the living room. His cheeks had color and his legs seemed stronger. Sitting there with Jenny, he looked like he'd taken twenty years off his age.

"I could watch her for hours," Tom said, never taking his eyes off his grandchild. "It's better than dessert."

"So you don't want dessert?" Elizabeth asked.

Tom suddenly looked up. "You made dessert?"

That night when she settled down in bed, Elizabeth took a moment to sigh. She had to admit all the new clothes, especially for Brady and Jenny, made a difference in her life. Every night since Brady had been born she'd gone to sleep worried that she couldn't provide for him. Then she'd added Jennifer.

She'd panicked when she'd learned about Reggie's death.

Their marriage had been over long ago, the love that she thought she'd felt for him long since dried up. She'd known what kind of man Reggie truly was, and that she'd made a huge mistake marrying him. Except that he'd given her children.

But when he died, she knew she had to take care of those children.

She should've checked about his bank account before she left for the Ransom Ranch. She knew Reggie had another checking account, because he'd sent her an occasional check from that account.

Maybe tomorrow she'd ask Tom about it. Maybe she could pay him back if she found out there was money remaining. Then she realized Tom would feel bad if she did that. So instead she'd merely offer.

She lay back against the soft pillows, glad for the silence in the monitor. A good night's sleep would be a luxury.

Not quite as much a luxury as it would be

to have some money, she thought. She looked around the room and her eyes settled on her dresser, filled with new clothes. With money, she thought to herself on a laugh, she could pick out her own underwear.

Jack.

The thought brought him to her mind.

The man drove her crazy.

She closed her eyes and went to sleep, strangely thinking of Jack seeing her in those black lace panties and matching bra he bought.

Elizabeth seemed awfully chipper the next morning as she cooked breakfast. Pretending to read the newspaper, Jack watched her without her knowing.

Her long light-brown hair was wavy and shiny, pulled back on one side with a clip to reveal her slender, creamy neck. Her cheeks had a rosy glow, her lips a soft pink hue, and the best part was that the color was all natural. No fussy creams and gels for this woman. With Elizabeth, what you saw was the real woman.

He imagined her with more curves on her thin frame, as she'd be after she stayed at the ranch for a while. He knew her life had been hard and she'd gone without, but now that Tom was taking care of her, she'd fill out— in all the right places.

The soft sound of her humming broke into his errant thoughts. She had a lovely voice and she nodded her head in the apparent beat of the song she intoned. The tune was familiar, but he couldn't place it.

He liked seeing her happy and made a mental note to tell Tom that his shopping trip had been a good one.

He too was pleased when Elizabeth sat down to breakfast. "I didn't know you'd be eating with me. It's a treat. Usually I eat alone." He dug in to the eggs and hash browns. "What do you have planned for today?"

"Some cleaning, in addition to cooking and taking care of my children."

"Aren't you going to church?"

"Of course, but I don't think I can take Jenny to Sunday School. Tom mentioned last night that he'd get up and go to Sunday School with Brady. He said you might—" she suddenly lowered the lids on her big blue eyes "—might take me and Jenny to church."

"I'd enjoy that. I don't always go to Sunday school, but I try to make it to church."

"We'll be ready on time."

He stared at her, wondering about her agreeableness. Then he said, "We'll be going out to lunch today, so you won't have to cook dinner."

That's when her agreeableness ceased. Her

head snapped up and she retorted, "But that's my job!"

"Tom and I usually go out to eat on Sunday."

"Yes, but now I'm here. That's what Tom is letting me do to pay him back for all he's given me."

"Tom thinks he's being nice because you gave him a reason to keep going." When she gave him a quizzical look, he explained. "Elizabeth, you and the kids are the reason he's getting out of bed. Before you came, he'd lost all hope."

She blinked, trying to deny the tears that clouded her voice. "He shouldn't have to pay for hoping. That's—that's sad."

"I agree, but that's how it was. I couldn't talk him out of bed half the days. He wanted to die. First his wife passed away, then Reggie left the ranch. He felt he had nothing left, no reason to keep the ranch going. He felt his life was over. But once you came, with the kids, he felt he finally had something to live for. Some hope for the future."

She whispered, "Brady."

"Yeah, Brady, but Jenny, too. He wants to regain his health, for both kids."

"What's wrong with him? Is there anything I can do?"

Jack shook his head. "That's the thing. Nothing's wrong with him. No medical problems at all. He's sixty-two and healthy as a horse. Except for his emotional malaise."

"But how can I help?"

"By giving him a chance. He's got plenty of money. That isn't important to him. Not like his grandchildren."

She smiled faintly. "I'm glad he feels that way. Brady's quite taken with him."

"I'm sure the feeling's mutual."

In fact, Jack had to admit the little boy had won him over too.

Just as his mother had.

When Jack came in from the morning chores, he quickly showered and changed into his church clothes. When he called down to Elizabeth and got no reply, he looked out the window and found her carrying Jenny to the pickup.

Grabbing his coat, he strode out to the trunk, eager to see her again and bask in her good mood. But when he saw her through the window, he came to an abrupt halt.

Something was wrong.

"What's the matter?" he asked as he got behind the wheel.

She didn't look at him but he could see the sadness on her face. It was mixed with confusion and anger and regret. "You tell me," she replied.

"What do you mean?"

After a moment she turned to him and he noticed her eyes were rimmed with red, as if she'd been crying. "Tom told me this morning you were planning on buying the ranch from him. Now he doesn't want to sell. He wants to keep the ranch for Brady."

He thought about his reply, then finally decided to tell her the truth.

There was no reason not to be honest.

He looked at her intently then, and on some level he noticed she was wearing one of the dresses he'd bought for her. She looked beautiful.

"Jenny is sure lucky."

That statement confused her. "What do you mean?"

"Jenny looks like you. That's why she's lucky."

"Thank you, but I want to know why you're

being so nice to me when I've ruined your life!"

He snickered and said, more to himself than to her, "I haven't figured that out yet myself.

"Look, Elizabeth, the land isn't going anywhere. And I'm still making the decisions about it. Tom doesn't have much interest anymore."

"But you won't own it!"

"I've been Tom's manager for almost ten years. I've been planning on buying it for five years. When I realized Reggie didn't have any interest in the place, it seemed like it was a prime property to buy." He shrugged. "It obviously didn't work out. Maybe I'll find another place and move on. I'm not sure what I'm going to do."

"But Tom can't manage without you!"

"That's not true. There are a couple of good cowboys who can manage the property."

"But Tom depends on you." Her voice hitched on a sob. "It just doesn't seem fair that his grandchildren and I have come into his life and now he has to lose you."

Jack nodded. He knew the feeling.

CHAPTER FOUR

RATHER than listen to the preacher, Elizabeth let her mind wander back to the conversation with Jack. She worried over Tom's decision to hold on to his property so he could give it to Brady.

She also worried about Jack.

It didn't seem fair for him to put in all that time on the ranch and then be denied it because a three-year-old arrived two days ago.

She thought she should do something for Jack. After all, he'd done his best for her.

When the congregation stood for a final

song, she joined in then took Brady's hand and led him out of the church. "You behaved very well this morning, sweetheart. And you look so handsome." Dressed in the sport coat and slacks Jack had picked out, Brady looked like a little man. "Did you enjoy yourself?"

"Yes, but it was kind of long, Mommy. And I'm real hungry."

She smiled at his candid assessment. "Jack said we're going out to eat." Though she didn't know why. She could cook a perfectly good meal at home. Maybe she'd talk to Tom.

When they got outside, Elizabeth waited for Tom and Jack to catch up with them.

"Tom, I don't mind cooking if you want to go home," she said.

"Nonsense, girl. It's a Sunday tradition for me and Jack. There's a good restaurant nearby we always go to. If we hurry up, we can get a table before they fill up." He leaned down to his grandson and ruffled his brown hair. "You ready, Brady?"

"Sure, Grandpa, but…what do you do when you eat out?"

"You tell the waitress what you want to eat, and she brings it to you."

"Wow! That sounds great."

"Actually, the food's not as good as your mom makes, but eating out is a nice change." He held out his hand and Brady put his hand in his grandfather's. But he sent a questioning look to his mother.

"You can go with Grandpa, sweetie. I'll ride with Jack and Jenny."

"Okay, Mommy."

She stood there watching him walk away with Tom, tamping down the emotion that threatened to overtake her. It was a welcome sight she feared she'd never get to see.

"Come on. We want to get a table."

She looked up in surprise at Jack. "Do we need to hurry?"

"Yeah, we do. And I need to tell you something else, too."

"What?"

"I'll tell you once we get in the truck." He reached down and took the baby carrier from her.

Once they were in the truck, she said, "What do you need to tell me?"

"Did you see the woman on the other side of Tom?" Jack asked as he started the truck.

"No, not really." The woman's car was on the far side of Tom's, hidden by his vehicle. She took Jenny out of the carrier to change her diaper.

"Her name's Carol. Tom was sitting with her in church. She's the lady who comes to clean our house. Tom doesn't want to stop that service. He wants you to not have to work so hard. And he knows Carol needs the money. She lost her husband about six years ago. That's how she supports herself."

"I see. I wouldn't want her to lose her job."

"Good. That will give you some time off."

She didn't think she needed time off, but arguing was useless.

Minutes later Jack turned into the parking lot of the restaurant. He came around to open her door. "I'll get the baby."

"That's okay. I can carry her."

"I've got her." He reached out with his other hand and caught Elizabeth's hand as she shut the door.

Having Jack hold her hand felt a little funny. At the same time she had to admit it felt good. Right. Exciting.

Brady was waiting in the lobby, sitting between his grandfather and the woman from church. Tom introduced Elizabeth to Carol

Johnson, an attractive blonde with a warm smile. Carol was eager to commend Brady on his behavior.

"I'm glad he behaved himself. I was sick most of my pregnancy with Jenny, so we didn't go to church much."

"I can understand that." The fifty-something woman nodded.

"How many children did you have?"

Carol shook her head. "I lost two babies midpregnancy."

"I'm so sorry." Elizabeth's heart went out to the woman. She couldn't imagine her life without her two babies.

Just then the hostess called their party.

"Come on, everyone," Jack said. As if it was a habit, he reached out and took Elizabeth's hand.

When he pulled out a chair for her at the table, Elizabeth had to admit this was a side of Jack she could easily get used to.

She sat down and reached out for the baby. However, Jack put Jenny in the upturned chair on the other side of his seat.

"But I need Jenny beside me."

"I'll take care of her today. Besides, that's where Brady is going to sit."

Before she could protest, Brady slid into the seat to her left, calling out to his grandfather to sit beside him.

Elizabeth studied the menu. "Everything sounds so good. I don't know what I want."

"I think you need a steak. You need some protein."

Irritated, she shot Jack a narrow-eyed look. "I do not!"

"Yes, you do. You need to gain some weight."

Darn that man! He had no idea how hard her life had been. From as far back as she could remember she'd had to be the responsible one, not only during her marriage but her childhood too. She'd taken care of her mother—who never knew Elizabeth's father—while the woman was strung out on crack. A habit she picked up working the streets of Oklahoma City.

Not much changed when she got married.

Even when she was terribly sick during her second pregnancy, she'd made sure to care for and feed Brady. Sometimes it was oatmeal with bananas—what she could make during the limited time she could stand up. One minute.

Jack Crawford had no right to judge her.

While she was stewing, the waitress arrived at their table and Jack immediately ordered a steak for her and for himself, too.

After the orders were in, Jenny made her presence known with a fussy cry. Elizabeth started to get up, but Carol, sitting beside Jenny at the circular table, asked her, "May I pick up the baby?"

"Yes, of course, Carol. But I can come get her when you want."

"Oh, I'd love to hold her. She's so little."

Jack assisted her in picking up the baby. "She may be little, but she's got healthy lungs."

"I didn't realize she was disturbing you," Elizabeth snapped.

"Come on, Liz, she's not bothering me. Not at all."

Elizabeth stared at the table, ignoring him.

"We love having little Jenny around. She reminds us about how lucky we are to have you and the kids come to our house." Tom looked at Brady. "Right, Brady?"

"Right, Grandpa."

"Do you have a bottle prepared?" Carol asked.

"Yes." Elizabeth bent down to the diaper bag and brought out a bottle for Jenny.

Carol fed the baby, cooing to her, smiling and obviously enjoying every moment of it.

"If you ever need a babysitter, Elizabeth, keep me in mind."

"Thank you, Carol, but I don't think I'll need a sitter." She had no intention of going anywhere without her children. Besides, where would she go?

"You never know," Jack said.

What was that supposed to mean? She was about to ask when the waitress appeared with their meals.

Elizabeth had had enough of this lunch and she hadn't even eaten yet. Still, she forced herself to eat, not wanting to hear any more of Jack's comments. He watched her throughout the meal as closely as she did Brady, only he made her uncomfortable.

She couldn't endure the ride back to the ranch with him.

"Tom, may Jenny and I ride back home with you and Brady?"

Jack heard her. "Aw, come on, honey, that's mean. That would leave me all alone."

"I'll ride with you, Jack," Brady said as he ate his ice cream for dessert.

"Good. I didn't want to ride alone. Thank you, Brady."

She couldn't very well forbid her son from riding with him. Especially not when the boy was so proud of his thoughtful gesture.

She sat back and drank her coffee.

When they finally got up from their meal, Jack picked up Jenny's carry-all.

"I'll take Jenny," she protested.

"Don't worry. I'll carry her to Tom's car."

Then he reached out to take her hand with his empty one, but Elizabeth sidestepped him. Instead she called out to her son. "Brady, be sure to wear your seat belt."

"I will, Mommy."

Carol said her goodbyes to Elizabeth, adding, "Feel free to rest today, Elizabeth. I'll be there tomorrow and I can pick up the slack."

"Thank you, Carol. It was so nice to meet you."

After they got in the car, Tom thanked her.

"For what?" Elizabeth asked.

"For being nice to Carol. She's a real friend."

"She seems very nice."

"She is. I'd marry her if I thought I'd be around long enough."

"I think you should marry her no matter how much time you have left. It's clear she cares about you. And she wouldn't be alone if she married you."

Tom seemed to give that some thought. "That's true, and I could leave her enough money, even if I keep the ranch for Brady."

Elizabeth realized this was the perfect opportunity to bring up her concerns. "Tom, I don't think you should worry about Brady. Jack—"

"You're right, Elizabeth." He nodded as he looked at her. "I can't forget about little Jenny. She wouldn't be happy with her grandpa."

He wasn't getting the point. "Tom, I can take care of my children."

"Yes, Elizabeth, you can. But I need to think about their future."

In Jack's pickup the two males were bonding.

Brady had numerous questions about Jack's life as a cowboy. "Can you ride a horse and shoot a gun?"

Jack laughed at the boy's version of a cowboy from the Wild West. "Yes, I can," he said. "Would you like to ride with me one day?"

"Can I?" His eyes were big as saucers.

"If your mom says okay."

Brady practically squirmed with excitement.

"Now it's my turn to ask you a question," Jack said. "Do you remember your apartment before you came to the ranch?" At the boy's nod, he continued. "Did you always have enough to eat then?"

"Oh, yeah. Mommy always made me eat."

"I'm sure she did. But did your mommy eat?"

Brady gave it some thought, tapping his finger against his head in the exaggerated gesture of a child. "Sometimes. But sometimes she didn't eat anything. Like when she had Jenny in her belly. She said she didn't want to throw up."

Just as he suspected, Jack thought. "That must've been hard. It's a wonder Jenny is all right."

"I asked Mommy if Jenny made her sick, but she said no."

"I think I'd better keep an eye on your mommy. Would you mind?"

"Nope, that's okay."

"I don't think your mom had a very good husband."

"Is that my daddy?"

"Yeah, buddy, that's your daddy."

"But my mommy said we needed him." His expression turned serious, and he turned his little body toward Jack. "She said we wouldn't have Jenny if we didn't have him."

The boy was right. And Jenny was worth it.

Jack shut his mouth and concentrated on his driving, laughing to himself at the irony. The rough-and-tumble cowboy had been taught a lesson by a three-year-old!

"Whose car is that?" Brady tore off his seat belt the minute the pickup came to a stop at the ranch.

"I don't know." Jack eyed the red Mercedes

with Texas plates. "Why don't you go on in and change out of your best clothes, son?"

Brady didn't even give the woman getting out of the car a look. He was on his way to wearing his jeans.

Jack stepped over to the young woman, dressed in tight designer jeans and a fuzzy vest and high-heeled boots. Clearly she was not from around here. "Are you lost, ma'am?"

"Is this the Ransom ranch?" she said with a Texas drawl.

"Yes, it is."

"Well, I'm looking for Mr. Tom Ransom." She smiled at him and gave him a once-over. "Is that you?"

He took a step back. "No, it's not. Here comes Tom now."

"Too bad."

When Tom's car stopped in the driveway,

Jack went around to the passenger side and reached in for Jenny.

"Who is that?" Elizabeth asked him.

"No one you need to concern yourself with. Go on in the house."

Something in his gaze must have told her to believe him because she didn't argue. "I'll take Jenny up and change her before she naps."

"I'll be in in a minute."

After she went in, Jack went around to Tom. "I think this lady is looking for you. I got a bad feeling about her."

"Is it someone I know?"

"No. I don't think so."

Tom got out of his car. "You looking for me, miss?" he asked.

"Are you Reggie's daddy?"

"Yeah."

She stepped forward and shot him a smile.

"Then, yes, I'm looking for you. You see, our Reggie is—was my husband."

CHAPTER FIVE

TOM and Jack stared at each other, their mouths agape.

Tom recovered first. "I see," he said in an even tone that belied the shock Jack knew he must have felt.

"It's too bad we didn't have more time together." She drew in a sharp breath and fluttered a manicured hand at her chest.

"Well, it was kind of you to come pay me a visit. Why don't we go in the house and get my housekeeper to serve us some cake. Don't you think that's a good idea, Jack?"

Jack couldn't help thinking Tom was

making a big mistake. The woman gave off some nasty vibes. But it was his ranch. "I guess."

"I'm sure it's a good idea. We have to offer something to this nice lady."

Jack followed behind them into the house. Once in the kitchen he offered to get Elizabeth. He found her upstairs in Jenny's room, patting the baby who lay on her belly in the crib. He touched Elizabeth on the arm and motioned to the door. She nodded and went out, pulling the bedroom door behind her after picking up the monitor.

"What is it, Jack?"

He could think of no way to explain the woman downstairs, so instead he said, "Tom wants you to come down and serve us all cake. Do you still have that chocolate cake?"

"Yes. But how could he want to eat again after that big lunch?"

"It's for…our guest. And don't be surprised when Tom doesn't introduce you."

She shot him a quizzical look but said, "Okay."

In the kitchen Tom was sitting at the table, along with the young woman from outside. Elizabeth tried not to stare at her as she got out the cake and plates. She cut three pieces of cake and served Tom, Jack and their guest.

"Aren't you going to have some cake, Elizabeth?" Jack asked.

"No, I'm not—"

"I think you should, Elizabeth." There was something in Tom's voice that intrigued her.

She sat at the table with a plate.

"I must say, you're very kind to offer your help, Mr. Ransom," the young woman said as she fluffed back her long, blond-streaked brown hair.

"Yeah, I'm a softhearted guy."

She leaned in closer to Tom and added, "Actually, though, you'd do better not to let her join us. They can get above themselves, you know."

"Oh, I don't think Elizabeth would get difficult."

Elizabeth said nothing, swallowing her anger with her cake.

The guest wasn't to be denied, however. "Was that her baby outside? I wouldn't think she'd be much good with a tiny baby. Surely, Mr. Ransom, you could find better help."

"Hey, that's a good idea. You can come live with me and be my housekeeper."

The woman nearly choked on her cake. "That's a joke, right?"

"No, I think it's a wonderful idea. You know, I don't feel very good sometimes. You could help me feel better."

"I don't know what you're talking about!"

"You know, cook me a good dinner, clean the house and do other things."

"I think you should keep—" she shot an affronted look at Elizabeth "—what was your name?"

"Elizabeth," she said.

"Why don't you use your full name, honey?" Jack interjected.

Elizabeth looked at him. What was going on here? Who was this woman?

Jack nodded his head, and Elizabeth went along. She turned to the young woman. "My name is Elizabeth Ransom."

"Tom's your father? I didn't know Reggie had a sister."

"He didn't."

"But you have to be his sister if your last name is Ransom."

"He was my husband."

The woman dropped her fork. "Don't be ridiculous!"

"I don't think I am," Elizabeth said with more calm than she felt. "He was my husband."

"When did he divorce you?"

"He didn't."

"He had to have. I mean, he went out with every woman who lifted her skirt!" She sized up Elizabeth with a glance. "Any woman with pride wouldn't have anything to do with him."

"So when did you marry him?" Jack asked the stranger.

Marry him? Elizabeth could feel her head spinning.

Beside her, Jack put his hand on her thigh under the table and patted her. What was he trying to tell her?

"A while ago," the woman replied.

"Before he married me?" Elizabeth asked.

"Well, I—"

Tom took over the questioning. "You weren't with him when he died, were you? But someone was with him. Another woman. That's a pretty short time to marry you and already have dumped you."

"He liked his freedom."

Tom nodded. "So I've heard." A few moments went by before he asked, "So why'd you marry him, then?"

"I hoped he'd settle down."

Elizabeth could understand that. Hadn't she fallen into the same trap?

The woman sounded almost pathetic when she added, "He even gave me a key to his apartment."

"Why?" Elizabeth asked.

"We were—we were in love."

Jack finally spoke up. "And did the key do you any good?" Jack asked.

"No, but maybe in time he would realize what— In time he would come around. I could feel him changing."

Elizabeth just stared at her, feeling sorry for her.

Jack apparently didn't share her emotion. She could detect a faint note of sarcasm in his tone when he told the woman, "Say, your car is nice."

The stranger obviously didn't pick up on it. "Thank you. Reggie gave it to me."

"He's got good taste. When did you get it?"

"I picked it up a week ago today. They had to verify that Reggie's check was good."

"Good to know you're not left broke," Jack said casually.

"Yes, it is," she said with a smile.

"How nice. But I guess the payments are high."

"Oh, no. Reggie bought it outright. He wouldn't want me to have to pay it out."

Jack nodded as he took in the information. "Say, Elizabeth, what car do you have?"

Elizabeth stared at him. "I didn't have a car."

"You mean Reggie left you with no car? How did you take Brady to the doctor?"

"We took a bus."

"Is Brady Reggie's kid?" the woman asked.

"Yes. And Jenny—the baby—is his, too."

The blonde's eyes widened. "So you have two children?"

Elizabeth answered, "Yes." Then she stood up and began clearing the table.

"Elizabeth, are you okay?" Tom asked.

"Yes, I'm fine, Tom. I'm going to go check on my kids."

"I think you made Elizabeth feel bad," Tom said to the woman after Elizabeth left.

A haughty look retook her face. "That wasn't my intention, but when you don't have any skills, you shouldn't have kids."

"Interesting observation." He looked up at the clock on the wall. "I'm getting tired, but I would like to talk more with you. Won't you spend the night, Miss…? I don't think I caught your name."

"Kim Hall."

"Wouldn't your name be Ransom?" Jack asked.

"I…I'm using my maiden name." Her cheeks flamed as she came up with a reason not to bear the name of her so-called husband.

"I hear that's popular."

Tom said, "I'm going to rest for a while, Jack. Can you entertain Kim for the afternoon?"

"Sure. Just wait until I go tell Elizabeth we'll have a guest for dinner."

Jack excused himself to trot upstairs. He found Elizabeth in her room.

"Are you okay?"

"Yes, of course."

"We'll be one more for dinner. I'm going to take our guest out to see the ranch. Then we'll come back and all have dinner."

"The kids and I will eat before you three. That way we won't interfere with your conversation."

"Elizabeth, you're not taking her seriously, are you?"

"Well, Reggie does—did have a reputation."

"Honey, you can't believe her. I'll stake my life on it that Reggie didn't buy that car for her. I suspect she signed one of his checks and took it to the Mercedes dealer after he died."

"Maybe Tom would rather have her here than me. She's very attractive."

"Nonsense. I know Tom. It took a while for me to figure out what he's doing. But it's that old adage 'Keep your friends close and your

enemies closer.' Tom's getting the information he needs, then he'll bring a lawsuit
against her. You'll see."

He leaned in close and kissed her on the
cheek. "You've got nothing to worry about,
Elizabeth."

When he left the room, Elizabeth knew that
wasn't true.

The innocent kiss had left a blazing imprint
on her skin. She touched her cheek and could
still feel his lips there.

She had a lot to worry about.

At six-thirty, Elizabeth had just put the finishing touches to a very good meal and called her
son to the table.

"You'll sit by me, sweetheart. And don't
worry about the stranger. I don't think she'll
pay any attention to you."

"Who is she?"

"A friend of your daddy's."

"Jack said my daddy was bad."

"No! He shouldn't have said that." She'd have to talk to Jack about that. "Your daddy was— Well, he didn't grow up, that's all."

"Will I grow up?"

She smiled at her son. "Of course you will, sweetie. You've already grown a lot. You always help when I need help, and you never complain."

"I'll help you anytime, Mommy." He threw his arms around her neck and squeezed her tight.

How she loved these spontaneous little-boy hugs. "Thank you, sweetheart. I always count on you."

"I'm hungry. When are they going to come?"

"I don't know. If you want to go out on the porch and look for them, you can. But don't get off the porch."

"I won't, Mommy."

Brady went out to the porch. After he went, Elizabeth thought about what she was going to tell Jack. She didn't want Brady to feel that there was something wrong with him. He was a good boy and he would be a good man.

By the time she had the roast on the table, Jack came in the door. "Sorry. Brady said we were late. Did we keep you waiting?"

"No, of course not."

"I intended to be in earlier but she—" he nodded toward the door and rolled his eyes "—wanted to spend some time with me." He snickered. "Yeah, right!"

"You didn't believe her?"

"No. She's only looking for a new fish to hook now that Reggie's gone."

"But surely she—" Elizabeth stopped talking as Kim came in the door. "Kim, will you knock on Tom's door, please?"

Kim frowned at her. "You want *me* to knock on his door?"

She looked at the woman, then she shook her head and walked past her to knock on Tom's door. "Dinner's ready, Tom."

Tom came out at once. "Glad to hear it. I was getting kind of peckish." He took a seat at the table. "This looks good, Elizabeth. This is what I'm talking about, Kim. Elizabeth here does a fine job of cooking and taking care of us."

"So she wouldn't get to eat if she didn't work?"

"Of course she would. But she willingly offered to keep the house and do the cooking. It's like she joined in with us, making life better. Believe you me, me and Jack got tired of those danged sandwiches."

"Well, you should have gone out to eat. That's what I would've done."

"Maybe," Jack said. "But you might not've had enough money."

"Why, I wouldn't have paid. Reggie always paid for me."

"There wasn't someone to pay when he was out with another woman. That must've made things difficult."

"Awkward might be a better word."

Elizabeth didn't like the conversation. She'd known women like Kim. She didn't like them then and she didn't like them now.

Looking for an excuse to call a halt to the line of dialogue, Elizabeth asked if Brady wanted more milk.

"No, thank you, Mommy. I'll wait for dessert."

He beamed at her, and she gave thanks for having such a good son.

Taking the shortcake out of the refrigerator, Elizabeth squirted whipped cream on each piece she cut and covered each with fresh-cut strawberries.

"This is great, Elizabeth!" Tom exclaimed when he took a forkful of his.

"Thank you, Tom."

"It is, honey. You did a great job." Jack sent her a special smile.

"Thank you." She looked at Kim. "I hope you like the dessert, Kim."

"It's fine but I would've preferred fresh whipped cream."

"It's great just like it is!" Tom said forcefully.

Kim stared at Tom, startled by his words. "Well, of course," she said as she gave Elizabeth a fake smile.

Brady reached out and claimed his mother's hand. "I like it the way Mommy made it."

"Thank you, Brady." Elizabeth squeezed Brady's hand.

Elizabeth couldn't wait to get away from

the dinner table and Kim. When dessert was finished, she reminded Tom of a TV program he wanted to watch.

Tom and Brady immediately got up from the table.

"Is that show all right for Brady to watch, Tom?" Elizabeth hurriedly asked.

"Sure is. They don't hardly even have any women, much less ones in skimpy clothes."

"All right. Mind your manners, Brady."

"I will, Mommy!"

Kim looked at the disappearing pair and then turned back to Jack. He, however, had begun carrying dishes to the sink. Finally, she said, "I guess I'll go watch television too." She paused at the door, apparently hoping Jack would offer her an alternative, but he didn't.

"I think you disappointed Kim," Elizabeth told him when Kim was out of earshot. "She was waiting for an invitation."

Jack looked at her blankly. "To do what?"

"I'm not sure, but I think she was hoping for something more romantic to do."

He snorted, an inelegant sound, but Elizabeth seemed pleased. "Unless I was paying through the nose, I don't think she'd be pleased."

They continued to work for a few moments before Elizabeth said, "Did you talk to Tom again about buying the ranch?"

"He sounded like his mind was made up."

"I'll talk to him. I don't think it's okay for you to be denied the right to buy the ranch just because Brady is here."

"That's what I like about you, Elizabeth. You don't just think of yourself. Or your kids."

"I favor my children, Jack. But I also know what's fair."

"Well, I like your style, but I can fight my own battles." He put away the last dish, then asked, "What do you have planned for the morning?"

"Nothing, other than fixing breakfast and doing laundry."

"I think you need to plan on coming to town with me."

"Why?"

"I'm going to the bank to open an account for you and transfer the contents of Reggie's bank account. I don't know how much was left, but you deserve it, not some woman who went out with him a couple of times."

"Do you think he has any money left?"

"He should have. He was winning a lot of rodeos."

"But shouldn't Tom have the right to the money?"

Jack shook his head. "As his wife, you're entitled to the money. Tom knows that."

"I'll go with you if you think it will help."

"Okay, we'll go at nine tomorrow and—"

"But I can't go then. I'll have to be here to fix Kim's breakfast. I don't think she'll be up early."

"First of all, you need to ignore Kim. Secondly, Carol will be here tomorrow. She comes in about seven, so she'll feed everyone after we leave."

"I forgot about her. That will be helpful."

"See? I told you that you had nothing to worry about."

Elizabeth stepped back from him. She didn't want another kiss to give her fantasies.

When Elizabeth got up at six, she immediately dressed and went downstairs to start Jack's breakfast. She knew he liked to go talk to the cowboys before he left the ranch for any period of time.

She also fixed her own breakfast. Breakfast

was nicer when it was shared. She smiled as she thought about the breakfasts she'd shared with Jack and Tom the last few days.

If they didn't have Kim intruding into their little family, she would be perfectly happy.

As she heard Jack coming downstairs, she brought two plates to the table.

"Morning, Liz."

"Jack, I've told you not to call me that. My name is Elizabeth."

"Didn't your family ever call you Liz or Lizzie?"

Her face shut down, her good mood flying off like a kite in the wind. She put his plate in front of him and turned away.

"Elizabeth?" She didn't respond to him. He tried again. "Honey, didn't you hear my question? Didn't your family ever call you nicknames?"

"No."

"Never?"

"No."

"You seem upset."

She walked over to the sink and threw her breakfast down the disposal. "When you finish, put your plate in the sink."

With her stomach rolling, she ran for the stairs and rushed up to hide away in her room.

Jack sat there in stunned silence. He'd known she'd been irritated when he called her Liz or Lizzie, but he hadn't expected such a harsh emotional reaction.

He thought about following her upstairs and asking for an explanation. But he was afraid to press her now. He'd try again when they drove into town.

Right now he had other things to occupy his mind, like disabling the Mercedes Kim drove to the ranch. He didn't want her trying to close the account that she'd already stripped of probably fifty thousand dollars.

He ate his breakfast and put his dishes in the sink. Then he went outside to the Mercedes, lifting the hood. After a couple of minutes, he took the battery out of the car and carried it into the barn.

Still, he couldn't keep his mind from Elizabeth. He hoped she'd come downstairs and answer a few questions.

He hated to think he'd hurt her.

When Jack got back to the house, he found a group circled around the table. Carol was there, as was Tom and Brady. And Elizabeth.

"Morning, everyone. Is there any leftover breakfast?"

"Are you hungry, Jack?" Carol asked, immediately standing up. "I can cook you some eggs and—"

"No, Carol, I ate breakfast earlier. I just thought you might have some leftovers. There's no need to cook anything."

"It won't take a minute. I've got pancake batter ready. I like to make them. Tom loves them."

"Yes, I do. Brady did a good job, too."

"Did Elizabeth eat some, too?"

Carol stared at Elizabeth. "She said she'd already eaten."

"I'm not hungry, Carol. I've just enjoyed visiting with you." She stood up. "Well, I guess we should get going."

Jack cut her off. "We'll leave in a few minutes. You need to eat first." He turned to Carol. "Would you please fix her a couple of pancakes?"

"I don't need—"

He ignored her irate look. "We're not leaving until you eat."

Jack quietly watched the struggle on Elizabeth's face. If she left, as he knew she wanted to do, she would hurt Carol's feelings. If she sat down again she'd feel he had won.

It wasn't a surprise to him that she agreed to eat just a little. He knew she wouldn't be rude to Carol.

He then initiated a conversation with Tom, hoping to divert attention from her so she could relax.

"Any sign of our guest?" he asked Tom.

"Nope. Carol checked on her before she started cooking. Still asleep."

"I don't think she'll be able to leave until I get back from the bank."

"Why?"

"I removed her car battery. I don't want her to leave until we've transferred whatever money is in the account." He paused to take a bite.

"Why would she leave money in the account?" Carol asked.

"I don't think she knew exactly what was there."

"Elizabeth, do you have any idea how much money is in Reggie's account?" Tom asked.

"No, Tom, I don't. I only know he had an account because he occasionally wrote me a check on it, but that's all I knew."

"Well, it's up to you. Just tell Jack what you want, and he'll make it happen."

Elizabeth stood and thanked Carol for the pancakes, then she cleaned her plate at the sink. She turned around to Jack. "Are we ready to go?"

"Yeah, we are."

She kissed her son. "Brady, be good while I'm gone."

"Okay, Mommy."

Jack knew Elizabeth would have a few

choice comments for him when they got to the car alone. He was ready for them.

"Jack, I don't want to take the car away from Kim."

That he definitely wasn't ready for. He shot her a confused look as he drove.

"I know she may have gotten it illegally," she said, "but I imagine Reggie took more than he gave."

"How do you know that?" Jack said, his voice full of irritation. He couldn't believe she was concerned about a lying gold digger who faked a marriage and scammed to get more money.

"Trust me, I know."

Reggie had no doubt done the same to her. But she was nothing like Kim Hall. He told her as much.

"You don't know that. You've only known me for three days."

Yeah, Jack said to himself, it was amazing,

wasn't it? "I know enough about you to know you're nothing like Kim. She's out to get what she can and she's not interested in giving anything. You, on the other hand, will give to anyone who needs something."

From the corner of his eye he saw Elizabeth look at him. He turned to her and grabbed her hand when the traffic came to a stop ahead of him.

"You're a good person, Elizabeth. And I aim to see you get what you deserve."

Her blue eyes glistened with tears and she ducked her head. "Thank you, Jack."

"Nothing to it."

They didn't speak again till they got to the bank.

Jack did the talking, explaining the problem to the bank president. He invited him into his office and opened an account for Elizabeth. Then he called the bank in Amarillo. He faxed them a copy of Reggie's death certificate and the papers from probate, which Elizabeth had supplied. He asked for the transfer of the funds available, telling whoever he was talking to that he had Reggie's widow sitting in his office. Jack asked for her marriage certificate and handed it to the banker.

Elizabeth was shocked that she so easily let Jack handle her business. But there was something about him that made her feel safe, taken care of. For the first time in her life.

But he also made her angrier than a bull seeing red, she reminded herself.

Caught in her daydream, she lost track of what the men were discussing. When Jack put a piece of paper in front of her, she stared at the figures on it, but they didn't really register.

"Elizabeth, what do you think of this balance?" Jack nudged her.

She forced herself to focus on the figure in

front of her, but the six figures kept fading in and out. It couldn't be. Reggie couldn't have left almost a quarter of a million dollars! Incredulous, she choked out, "This is the balance right now?"

"Yeah, that's before we recover the money for the car."

As if snapped out of a trance by a hypnotist, she felt her head clear. "I told you I didn't want to take the car away. It's not something I want to drive."

"If you don't take the money away from her, you'll be allowing her to get away with fraud," the banker explained.

"I don't want the car and I don't want to bring charges against the woman. I'm sure she won't do that again."

Jack commiserated with the banker, and they whispered together while Elizabeth sat quietly and took in the new developments.

Two hundred fifty thousand dollars.

Never in her life did she ever think to see that much money. And now she owned it all.

"Elizabeth, what do you want to do with the money?"

She gave Jack and the banker a blank look.

The bank president leaned forward. "My advice would be to put the bulk of it in high-yield investments and the remainder in an interest-bearing checking account."

That sounded good to her.

"How about we keep ten thousand in the checking?" the banker suggested. "Is that enough for you?"

She looked at him as if he were crazy. "More than enough."

"In that case, then, I think we're finished here. We'll send you your checks when they're printed, but in the meantime you can use these." He handed her a few generic checks and stood up. "A pleasure to meet you, Mrs. Ransom."

Shaking his hand, she returned the compliment.

When they exited the bank, her head was still spinning at the money at her disposal.

"How are you feeling?" Jack asked her.

"I'm not sure really." She turned to look at him. "Jack, do you promise to leave Kim alone?"

"Yeah, but why are you protecting her? She doesn't care about you."

"I know that, but…but we were victimized by Reggie. She deserves something."

"So you're going to let her get away with it?"

"Yes, and I'm tired of talking about it."

"But it's a lot of money."

"Yes, it is. And I have a lot of money now, myself. I can afford to let her have it." To terminate the conversation, she walked ahead, leaving Jack standing outside the bank.

Elizabeth was eager to break the news at home. When they got to the ranch she found Kim sitting by herself at the kitchen table. "Do you know where Carol is?"

"Never mind that," she said with a sharp tone. "What did Jack do to my car? It won't start, and Tom said Jack did something to it."

"Jack thought you should remain here until we got things straightened out at the bank."

"What are you talking about?"

"We had the bank transfer Reggie's money to my account."

The blonde nearly lost control. "You can't do that! That's my money!"

Despite her outburst, Elizabeth remained in control. "We didn't report your theft of the car you bought, Kim, but you should calm down.

I understand that Reggie betrayed you, too. But the kids need the money their father earned."

"But he was going to marry me! I deserve that money!"

The woman was so loud, Tom and Brady came out of Tom's room. Carol hurried down from upstairs and Jack came in after fixing Kim's car as he'd promised.

Faced with so many people who had little interest in her position, Kim appeared to think she should get louder rather than quieter.

Elizabeth tried to reason with her, but she refused to listen.

Jack didn't see any need for sympathy. "Face it, Kim. You stole fifty thousand dollars that didn't belong to you. Because of Elizabeth's generosity and sympathy, she's letting you keep the car. But the rest of it is hers."

"I have more checks!"

"It doesn't matter. If you try to pass another check on that account, you'll be arrested and put in jail."

She stared at him, obviously overwhelmed. "But what should I do? I have to have a man to support me! Reggie promised to take care of me!"

"You're going to have to find someone else to take care of you. Reggie can't anymore."

Jack sounded so stern that Elizabeth felt like crying herself.

Kim, on the other hand, got meaner. "You can't tell me what to do! I'll find a way to get that money! It certainly doesn't go to her just because she had a couple of kids!" Then she paused long enough to take a breath and turn to Elizabeth. "I think I'm pregnant, too!"

CHAPTER SIX

EVERYONE froze, staring at her.

Brady looked at his mother. "What did she say?"

Realizing her young son shouldn't hear this conversation, Elizabeth hunkered down to his level. "Sweetheart, would you go check on your sister for me? And then you can play in your room till Mommy comes up."

A good boy, Brady did as he was asked.

Tom wasted no time. As soon as Brady turned away he asked Kim, "When were you last with my son?"

"About six weeks ago."

"Have you been to a doctor?"

"No! I mean, I didn't see the reason to—No, I haven't been to the doctor."

"You aren't pregnant," Jack said in disgust.

"I could be!"

"Come on, I'll take you to the doctor," Jack said gruffly.

"No! I'll go to my doctor at home."

Before anyone could waver, Jack held their ground. "I don't think we should let her go until we get her checked out by Doc."

Kim remained adamant. "I don't want to go to a strange doctor."

Elizabeth could understand that. She led Kim to a chair at the table. "I think we all need to sit down and discuss this quietly."

She remembered Reggie's reaction to her pregnancy with Jenny. He'd blown up at her, accusing her of lying, of tricking him. He'd vowed not to be trapped again, as he said he'd been with Brady. His callous reaction had hurt her immeasurably and she'd never forget how she cried.

Still, she knew one thing for sure: Reggie would never risk pregnancy again.

And she didn't think he had this time.

"Look, Kim, Jack is just trying to help. I'm sure he didn't mean to sound so gruff."

Jack glared at Elizabeth. She ignored him and kept her gaze on Kim. "I know you must be uncomfortable talking about this, but we need to know. Did you have unprotected sex?"

"Not usually. Reggie was careful, but…but he forgot sometimes."

"And you forgot, too?"

"Yes. I wanted to— I mean, I'm sure it was an accident, but—"

"I think we can settle this with a simple home pregnancy test." She looked up at Jack. "Jack, could you go buy one?"

"Yeah," he muttered.

He stalked out of the house, leaving everyone silent.

Elizabeth asked Carol to put on some water for hot tea.

Kim protested. "I'll just have coffee."

"You really shouldn't have coffee if you're pregnant." Elizabeth smiled. "I know. I hated giving up my coffee."

"And you did? Did your doctor insist? For the entire pregnancy?"

"Yes, I'm afraid so."

"I didn't know that." Kim sat quietly for a moment, then she looked up at Elizabeth with frightened eyes. "I don't think I want to be pregnant."

"We'll keep our fingers crossed," Elizabeth said as she patted the woman's hand.

Jack felt like a fish out of water.

He stood in the middle aisle of the town

pharmacy scratching his head as he gazed out on an array of choices. There had to be fifteen different home pregnancy kits.

He knew about cattle, about horses, tack and grain. But what did a cowboy know about pregnancy tests?

"Can I help you, Jack?"

Mrs. Johnson's voice echoed through his thoughts.

Just what he needed. Old Mrs. Johnson had been working in the pharmacy since Jack came to town ten years ago. She'd helped him through flu and colds, broken fingers and sore shoulders.

How was he going to ask her for this?

"Hello, Mrs. Johnson. I—I was looking for some more liniment."

"You're sure, Jack? You're standing in front of pregnancy kits." She paused to give him time to answer. Then, with a once-over that burned him through his clothes, she put on her half-glasses and perused the shelf.

She chose a box and handed it to him.

"This one's the best, I'm told. Just in case you need it."

Jack prayed for an early death.

Elizabeth took the sack from him as soon as Jack came into the kitchen. "If you'll come with me, Kim, we'll have an answer."

She led the blonde upstairs to a more private bathroom, went over the instructions and left her to do her thing.

Leaning against the opposite wall in the hallway, Elizabeth kept looking at her watch as her mind raced. As kind as she could be, she had to admit she didn't want the woman to be pregnant. Not because of the money, but because her children would forever be tied to Kim. They'd have a half sibling who lived with her. And Kim Hall was not the kind of woman she wanted her children associating with.

She checked her watch again. The box said it took only two minutes. What was taking so long?

Just then the bathroom door opened and Kim stood there, her face void of emotion.

Elizabeth could hardly speak. "Well?" she managed.

"I'm not pregnant."

Keeping her relief in check, she wrapped an arm around Kim's shoulders. "We should tell the others."

Elizabeth offered to make the announcement when they reentered the kitchen, but Kim shook her head. Almost magically her personality changed back to the nasty witch from earlier. She stood with arms akimbo and shrugged.

"I'm not pregnant. Satisfied?"

"Yeah, I'm satisfied," Jack said. "It was worth going to the drugstore and ruining my reputation!"

Elizabeth stared at him. "What do you mean?"

"Never mind."

"Well, there's no reason for me to stay," Kim said, already heading for the door. She turned, as if remembering something. Shooting a deadly glare at Jack, she asked, "Does my car work now?"

"Yeah."

Kim was on her way after that response.

After the click of the door lock, silence descended upon the kitchen.

Elizabeth felt relieved, and she suspected Tom was, too. But no one wanted to be the first to express the emotion.

As she looked up at her father-in-law, Jenny's cry broke the stalemate.

"That's Jenny. She's probably hungry." She noticed that Carol seemed anxious. "Do you want to go get her, Carol? Just change her diaper and bring her down. I'll get her bottle ready."

"Bring her down, Carol." Tom looked happy at the thought of holding his granddaughter.

After Carol left the room, Jack looked at Elizabeth. "Why did you let her go get Jenny?"

"I thought she deserved to get her. She'd taken care of Brady and Tom and helped entertain Kim. It only seemed fair that she get to take care of Jenny."

"That was nice of you, Elizabeth," Tom said.

"Carol is a nice lady."

"Yes, she is," Tom agreed.

They all heard Carol coming down the stairs, followed by Brady.

Elizabeth hugged her son. "Hi, sweetie. Thank you for being such a good boy."

"He was patting his little sister on the back," Carol said. Her smile said she was proud of Brady, too.

"Carol said I was helping," Brady told his mother.

"Yes, you were, honey."

She handed the bottle, properly warmed, to Carol. "Do you mind feeding her while I finish preparing lunch?"

"No, I'd love to." Carol took the bottle. "I was hoping you'd be gone when she woke up. Now I get the best of both worlds."

"You deserve it, Carol," Elizabeth said.

"What about me?" Tom said. "I had to act nice when that lady talked about being pregnant."

"We've all had a difficult day," Jack said with a sigh.

"Lunch will be ready in a few minutes. Anyone want a cup of coffee?"

"Yeah, that would be good," Jack said. Tom nodded, too.

Elizabeth poured coffee for the two men. She poured some juice for Brady. Then she began fixing some vegetables to go with the casserole.

When Carol finished feeding Jenny, Tom moved over to visit with Carol and the baby. She put Jenny in his arms, and he cooed at her, patting her smooth cheek and letting her grab his pinky as he did so. "I'm your grandpa, Jenny. Grandpa Tom."

The baby's eyes were wide as she listened to her grandfather.

"She seems mesmerized," Elizabeth said. "I guess maybe because she doesn't hear a man's voice very often. It's just been me and Brady around her since she was born."

"We'll have to change that, right, Jack?" Tom asked without taking his eyes off his granddaughter.

"Yeah, we will. She needs to get used to both of us."

Elizabeth didn't say anything.

Jack had served himself and started eating, but he noticed that Elizabeth didn't come down after taking Jenny back upstairs. After a few moments he excused himself and went to get her. He found her in Jenny's room, slowly rocking the sleeping baby.

Instead of saying anything to Elizabeth, he sat down on the small bed and waited a minute. Then he called her softly. "Elizabeth?"

Her eyes opened and she cleared her throat before finally responding. "Yes, Jack?"

"I wondered when you were coming down for lunch. It's getting cold."

"I was just rocking Jenny."

"She seems sound asleep. I'll put her in her bed."

Elizabeth wanted to protest, but he was being helpful.

After he'd put the baby down, he pulled her up from the rocker and led her out of the baby's room. "Were you planning on skipping lunch?"

"No, but it's so peaceful, holding a sleeping baby. Today had a lot of disturbing situations."

"Yeah. I'm glad you thought of the pregnancy test."

"I'm sorry it caused you some embarrassment."

"It irritated me most of all."

"I'm glad we now know."

"Yeah, she didn't seem the mothering type."

"People change. She might have turned into a good mother."

"Yeah, right." He took her hand and led her down the stairs.

"Did you think I couldn't find the table without your assistance?"

"You seem all too ready to skip meals. I think you need to eat a good lunch."

When they entered the kitchen, Carol made her a plate and Tom pulled out a chair for her.

"What is everyone going to do this afternoon?" she asked as she sat.

"I'm going to be sure you eat your lunch."

"Jack, you don't need to help me."

He just looked at her but he didn't budge from the chair opposite her.

Carol offered her plan. "I'm going to actually do some work. I didn't get anything done besides making the beds."

"There's too much else needed, Carol. I think you should relax and entertain Tom. Brady is going to take his nap, and Tom won't have anyone to talk to."

"Aw, Mommy, I don't need a nap," Brady said as he tried to hide a big yawn.

Everyone chuckled.

"I'll come up and cover you up, sweetie."

Jack spoke up. "Not until you finish your lunch. I'll go tuck him in."

When she started to protest, Brady expressed enthusiasm about Jack helping him. So she remained seated as the two males went upstairs together.

"That was nice of Jack," Carol said.

Elizabeth said nothing.

"Do you have some laundry ready to be washed?" Carol asked her. "I could do some laundry for you."

"Yes, I do. You always have laundry when you have children."

"I've heard that," Carol said, a wistful look in her eyes.

Poor Carol had never had children after losing two babies. Elizabeth's heart went out to her. She felt even more grateful for her children.

"Do you need to get home early tonight, Carol, or will you stay for dinner?"

Carol turned bright red. "You don't have to include me for dinner."

"You always stay for dinner, Carol," Tom said. "Though I appreciate you asking her, Elizabeth."

"I'd love to stay, Elizabeth. Thank you."

"Okay, I'll get started on cleaning the kitchen, if you'll gather the laundry. Be sure to look under Brady's bed."

"Just like the other two men!" Carol chuckled.

"Hey, we try," Tom assured both women.

"We know," Elizabeth said.

Jack knocked quietly on Tom's door.

"Tom, are you asleep?"

"No. Come in."

Jack opened the door and found him in the wing chair. "I was thinking about Christmas.

Brady was telling me about not having had a Christmas tree yet. He said his mommy promised that one day they'd have one."

"He's never had a Christmas tree?" Tom asked, incredulous.

"Yeah," Jack said. "I told him maybe we could have a tree this year. I was thinking tonight after dinner would be a good time to go shopping for one."

"Good thinking. Shall we keep it a secret? We could decorate it tonight, too."

"I think that would be good. We can show Elizabeth what we have and maybe she could buy what else we need."

Tom smiled. "I'm so glad they've come. It will be fun to have a real Christmas again."

"You will, Tom. You'll have a Christmas and so will Elizabeth and the kids. I'll make sure of it."

* * *

"A Christmas tree!"

Brady could hardly contain his excitement when Jack mentioned the possibility of going for a tree that night after dinner.

"Where do we go to get one?" Brady asked him.

"At the Christmas tree lot in town. Do you want to go?" Jack asked casually.

"Can I, Mommy? Please?"

"I don't know, Brady. Maybe they want to pick out their tree without us—"

"It will be *our* Christmas tree, Elizabeth," Tom said.

"And I think Brady would give good advice about the tree," Jack said. "In fact, as cold as it is, I'm not sure Tom wants to wander around looking at all the trees."

"Won't it be too cold for Brady?" Elizabeth asked anxiously.

"No. I'll keep an eye on him."

Jack waited for her response.

After a quick look at Brady, Elizabeth agreed that her son could go. "Go get your coat and hat and gloves, Brady, and bring them to me."

"Any requests?" Jack asked.

"Yes," Tom said. "I think you should invite Elizabeth to go. I'll help Carol clean the kitchen and we'll babysit Jenny."

"Oh, no!" Elizabeth protested. "I wanted Carol to stay so she could enjoy a nice meal, not to babysit."

"I think you should go," Jack said. "We might need help choosing the right tree."

Brady came running down the stairs, holding his coat, gloves and hat out to his mother.

"I think she's going with us, Brady, so we can get the best tree possible."

"You're going, too, Mommy?" Brady asked, his eyes lighting up even brighter.

"Well?" Jack added.

"Yes, I'll come if Carol doesn't mind. But you can leave the dishes for me to do. Jenny will be up soon."

"We'll see."

Brady would've taken the first tree they looked at. Jack cautioned him to look at a few more before he made his decision.

Amidst the delicate snow flurries floating in the cold night, Elizabeth wandered the tree-filled stands, her eyes as bright as Brady's. When Jack saw her pause by a stately Frasier fir and circle it, checking it from every angle, he leaned down and suggested Brady go look at the tree his mother had found.

"Mommy, do you like this one?"

"I love it, Brady, but I think it might be too big."

"I think it'll be perfect," Jack said, coming

up behind her. He signaled the man running the tree farm. "We'll take this one, Jonas."

"Good choice, Jack. That's the best tree I have this year."

Brady beamed up at Jack. "We picked a good one, didn't we?"

Jack patted the boy on his back. "We definitely did."

"What do we do now?" Brady asked Jack.

"We pay for the tree, and Jonas here will trim the bottom off so it will soak up the water. Then we'll put it in our truck and drive it home."

Elizabeth stepped up and Brady put his arms around his mother, as far as his little arms could go. "Mommy, we've got our first Christmas tree!"

She bent down and hugged Brady. "Yes, we do, Brady, thanks to your grandfather…and Jack."

Standing there with the snowflakes falling

around them, mother and son looked so content, so beautiful that Jack couldn't take his eyes off them.

They looked like an advertisement for the holiday season.

The perfect family.

Only one thing was missing. A dad.

CHAPTER SEVEN

EVEN though they didn't decorate the tree that evening, Brady was still excited. Elizabeth was, too, though she tried not to admit it.

Jack watched both of them, enjoying their excitement. He and Tom hadn't bothered with much Christmas in the past couple of years. After losing his wife, and then his son turning his back on him, Tom never seemed to be in the holiday spirit.

Nor had Jack.

He hadn't even gone back home the last few Christmases.

It wasn't that he wouldn't have been

welcome. It just seemed so much easier to stay at the Ransom Ranch. Besides, Jack needed him.

Now, though, he realized how much they'd missed. Now that they had someone to share Christmas with.

They put the tree in a bucket of water in the barn. Even though it was cold, Brady stood there, staring at the tree, as if he thought it might jump up and start dancing around.

"Brady, you need to come in now. It's cold out here." Jack reached out to take the little boy's hand. "Come on, let's go inside."

"But I think our tree might get lonely."

"No, sweetie, trees won't get lonely. You can come see it tomorrow morning, if you wear your coat and gloves."

"Okay, Mommy."

Jack took his hand and led him to the house.

"Oh, I'm glad you've come in. There's a

Christmas special on television," Carol exclaimed as they came into the house. She was carrying Jenny, warming up her bottle.

"Go on back to the television room, Carol. I'll bring Jenny's bottle as soon as it's warmed," Elizabeth said.

"Okay, but I'll let you feed her. You haven't spent much time with her."

"Thank you, Carol," Elizabeth said.

Brady had already run to the television, joining his grandfather. He shouted to Elizabeth, "Mommy, it's Frosty the Snowman."

"Brady still sounds excited." Jack was taking off his coat in the kitchen, hanging it on a peg by the door.

"He'll probably be excited until Christmas is over," Elizabeth said. The timer on the microwave beeped, indicating the bottle she'd put was ready.

"Here, let me have your coat," Jack said, holding out his hand.

"Thank you." She slipped out of her coat and handed it to him. Then she took the warm bottle and went into the television room. He followed her in.

Carol handed over Jenny, and Elizabeth settled in an upholstered chair and began feeding Jenny, talking to her about the Christmas tree they'd bought.

"Next year she can go with us."

Elizabeth jerked her head up to find Jack standing beside her chair. "I didn't know you were there."

"I didn't want Jenny to think we'd forgotten her."

"She's too little to go to buy a tree this year, but I wanted her to know that next year we won't leave her at home."

"That's right, little Jenny. I'll be sure to take you."

Jack perched on the arm of the chair and continued to chat with Jenny. Her big blue eyes stared right at his face, following his every movement.

Elizabeth listened to Jack, too, hoping against hope that what he said was true. That there'd be a next year for them all to get a Christmas tree together. That they'd go see Santa and write a wish list to give him.

She had a wish list. She wished that Jack had been her husband, not Reggie. Jack wouldn't have been unwilling to claim their daughter, as Reggie had. He wouldn't have ignored his children, his wife.

She'd never understood Reggie. But she did understand that she'd never marry again. Not when her first marriage had been such a disaster.

The only good that had come out of her marriage were her children.

Now she would be able to take care of them the way they deserved. To be the kind of mother she'd always wanted to be. With the money transferred to her name she could stay home until Jenny went to school.

While she'd been thinking, she realized Jenny had finished her bottle.

Taking the bottle from Jenny's mouth, she patted the baby on her back and burped her until she had success. Then she got up from the chair and carried the baby upstairs.

When she returned, her son was asleep on his grandfather's shoulder. She leaned down to take him upstairs, but Jack stopped her.

"I'll take him upstairs."

"But he's got to get undressed. I'll come up with you."

Once they reached Brady's room, Elizabeth

found his pajamas and changed him without waking him up.

"Man, he's a deep sleeper," Jack said.

"Yes, he is," Elizabeth said with a smile.

"How did you manage while you were pregnant?"

"We didn't go out often."

"I don't guess Reggie came to see you?"

"No. Especially not with the second pregnancy."

"Why?"

"Because he didn't want Jenny."

"I don't think that's how babies are created."

"Don't tell Reggie that."

"I think it's a little late to tell him anything."

"Yes, I guess so."

She pulled the cover up over Brady and leaned down to kiss him good-night.

Jack waited until she was ready to leave Brady's bedroom.

"Do you need help cleaning the kitchen?"

She shook her head. "Carol did it all."

"That's what she gets paid to do."

"I think I need to pay her salary."

"I think that's Tom's job. He likes paying her."

Elizabeth smiled. "I think he's interested in her."

"What do you mean?"

"He told me he would've married her a while ago if he hadn't been feeling so bad." She tilted her head. "But he seems to be feeling better now."

"Yeah, I think you're right. The kids have given him a lift."

"I'm glad he's getting something out of us coming here. I need to talk to him about paying rent."

"You can't do that!"

She turned to stare at him. "Why not?"

"He wants to provide for you and the kids. His son obviously didn't."

"But he did. He just didn't intend to. So I should pay rent."

"But who'll cook if you're paying rent?"

She looked confused. "I will, of course."

"We can't let you cook and clean. Not if you're paying to live here."

It'd been such a lovely evening, but now Jack was pushing her again, telling her what to do. "I'm going to ask Tom." She stomped to the television room. "Tom, you don't mind my cooking and cleaning, do you?"

"Wait a minute, Tom, before you answer," Jack said. "She's talking about paying for living here, *and* cooking and cleaning."

Tom frowned. "Why would you do that?"

She tried to ignore Jack. "Now that I have Reggie's money, I feel like I should pay you something."

"I don't want your money, Elizabeth, but I sure can use your cooking."

"But—"

"I think this argument is over." Jack reached out to catch Elizabeth's hand. "You can't argue with the man."

She threw off his touch. "We wouldn't be arguing if you hadn't interrupted us."

"I wouldn't have interrupted if you had told the whole story. Now, Lizzie—"

"Don't call me that!"

"I can't believe your family didn't call you Lizzie!"

Something inside her snapped. Before she could stop herself she blurted, "I didn't have any family! I was taken away from my mother because she was addicted to drugs. I was five and that's the last time I ever saw her! I don't even know who my father is."

Jack frowned. "You weren't adopted?"

"Would you want to adopt a child whose mother was an addict?"

"You didn't take the drugs. Why not?"

"They only want babies. They—" Tears filled her eyes, stinging them, threatening to spill over. "It doesn't matter anyway." Spinning on her heel, she walked toward the steps.

Jack's words stopped her.

"You're a good mother, Elizabeth. You're nothing like your mother."

The tears flowed freely then, and she could do nothing to stop them.

Tom took her in his arms. "You deserved better than Reggie, but maybe it turned out well, after all. We can be a family, all of us here."

She looked up at him and wiped her tears away. "I'd like that, Tom."

He smiled at her. "Good. And our family is growing even more. I've just asked Carol to marry me."

She hugged him. "I'm so happy for both of you."

Carol looked at Elizabeth. "You don't mind if I come live here?"

"Not at all, Carol. That will be wonderful! I've learned that you can never have too much family." Elizabeth hugged the woman.

"When are you going to marry?" Jack asked as he shook Tom's hand.

"Whenever Carol is ready."

"I'm ready now," she said without hesitation.

Tom beamed at her. "Then let's get married Friday night."

"We'll need to get a wedding cake," Elizabeth said. "Is there anyone we can call to bake a wedding cake?"

"Yeah, but Jack will have to call her," Tom said. "She always agrees when Jack calls her."

Elizabeth looked at him. "Well?"

"Sure, I'll call her."

"Good." Elizabeth turned to go upstairs. "If you'll excuse me, then, I've got to go check on the children." She walked quickly up the stairs.

"I don't think your little joke went over well," Jack said ruefully when she was out of earshot.

Tom shook his head. "I'll tell her what I meant in the morning."

"You'd better." He said his good-nights. "I'm leaving you two alone. Stay out of trouble!"

On the way to his room, he was tempted to knock on Elizabeth's door, but he didn't think she'd listen to him. He hadn't spoken up when she'd confessed to not having a family. But he'd wanted to.

He'd wanted to rush to her, hug her and let her know that she would have made any parent proud, that she had people who loved her, even though she hadn't had a family till now.

But he hadn't.

Instead, Tom had stepped up and hugged Elizabeth and made her feel like she was a part of the family.

What had held him back?

Fear.

He was afraid he was falling in love with Elizabeth.

Jack felt hung over when he got up the next morning when the alarm went off. But it wasn't booze that had given him trouble. It was a woman.

The woman he'd heard walking the hallways last night as he lay awake.

Elizabeth, too, had had a bad night sleeping.

When he entered the kitchen he saw that she'd fixed his breakfast—her pancakes, his favorite—and left them covered on the stovetop. But there was no sign of her.

He knew he had to rectify the assumption she'd made last night, or else she'd be mad at him all day.

He ate his breakfast and thought about how he would handle the situation.

On the one hand Elizabeth was the most understanding woman he'd ever met. On the other hand, she was also the most stubborn. There was really one way to clear up the misunderstanding.

She had to come with him to order the cake.

He went upstairs and gently knocked on her door. When there was no response, he put his ear against the wood and listened. Hearing nothing, he tried the bathroom door, but with no results.

Either she was still asleep or she was totally ignoring him.

Because he had to meet up with the hands and issue the day's instructions, he put her on hold and went out to tend to the ranch. Elizabeth was never far from his mind, and the first spare moment he had he came back to the house. He found her in the kitchen making another pot of coffee.

"Good morning."

She merely responded in kind, but didn't turn from her task.

Next he ventured, "Elizabeth, will you go with me to order the cake today?"

Her hand froze. "I don't think that will be necessary."

"You could explain what Carol wants much better than I can."

She cast him a look over her shoulder. "But—"

He gave her the brightest smile he could muster. "Great. We'll go in an hour." Then he walked out of the kitchen, whistling to himself.

* * *

Elizabeth had fed and changed Jenny by the time Jack came back in an hour later. How had she gotten herself roped into going with him?

It was for Carol, she told herself.

"Are you ready?" Jack asked as he stepped out of the washroom. "Where's Jenny?"

"The kids are with Tom in his room. Brady's watching TV."

"Then let's go." He went to help her with her coat, but she took it from him and put it on herself.

She was quiet on the ride, not initiating any conversation and offering only limited responses to his attempts.

"The cake lady doesn't live too far away," Jack said after he pulled away from the house.

"Good."

"Are you busy today?" he asked.

"No more than usual." Her reply was polite but clipped, and she kept her gaze straight ahead.

"I wanted to thank you for coming with me."

"I did it for Carol, not you."

Finally Jack took the hint, and they rode the rest of the way in silence.

A few minutes later Jack pulled into the driveway of a charming farmhouse. He led her around back and opened the door into the kitchen. "Edith?" he called, since no one was in sight.

They both heard a faint "Coming!"

She could've sworn Jack chuckled beside her as they stood there waiting for the baker to arrive.

When she saw the small figure enter the kitchen she knew why.

The cake lady was seventy, if she was a day.

Elizabeth shot Jack a look and he bared his white teeth in a huge smile as he laughed.

"Jack!" The old woman threw her arms

around him, her tiny frame dwarfed by his large one.

"Hi, Edith. How are you doing?"

"I'm fine. What can I do for you?"

"Tom's getting married this Friday. I know it's short notice, but we were hoping you could manage to make a wedding cake for him."

She looked at Elizabeth for the first time. "Who's this? Is she the bride?"

Elizabeth had to stifle a laugh. "No! I mean, no, I'm not the bride. It's Carol."

"Oh, good." Edith gave her an assessing once-over. "So who are you?"

"I'm Tom's daughter-in-law."

"Reggie's wife?" Edith asked in horror.

"Reggie's widow."

"Oh, poor Tom." Then she turned back to Jack and her demeanor changed. "So he's finally going to marry Carol? That's good. How many people?"

"We figure a couple of hundred," Jack said.

"What style cake do you want?"

Jack looked at Elizabeth. "That's your job."

Elizabeth described it, and was a bit concerned when Edith didn't write anything down.

"Got it. I'll have it ready Friday by noon."

Jack thanked her. "We would've given you more time, but he didn't ask her until last night."

"A couple of romantics, eh?"

"Yeah, I guess they didn't want to waste any time," Jack said with a grin.

"I don't blame them. They're not getting any younger." She gave Jack a smile, and Elizabeth swore she saw the woman bat her eyelashes at him.

Jack stepped back, a fearful look on his face. "I…I'll see you Friday."

He got out of the farmhouse before Edith

could kiss him goodbye. Elizabeth could only laugh as she followed.

When they got to the truck, he shot her a look. "I don't think it's funny. Sometimes that woman scares me."

She tried to stop laughing. "I'm sorry." When she sobered, she said, "I'm also sorry for thinking you were dating Edith."

"Thank you."

She shrugged. "It's none of my business anyway."

"What do you mean?"

"It means that I have no right to be concerned about who you date. You're a single man with no ties. You can date whomever you want."

Jack nodded at her comment, apparently in agreement. But the thought struck her as untrue.

It did bother her who Jack dated. But why?

Because she was jealous.

Because she cared about him.

Because, she realized with a gasp, she was falling for him.

When they arrived back at the ranch, Jack went straight to Tom. They had important business to discuss.

Elizabeth followed him and immediately went to Brady, who was sitting on the floor, playing cards with Tom. "Brady, is everything all right?"

"Sure, Mommy. Jenny's asleep and we're playing cards."

"I didn't know you knew how to play."

"Grandpa taught me."

Tom seemed pleased. "Jenny's upstairs asleep."

"I'll just take Brady and go check on her." Elizabeth ushered her son out of the room. "I'll let you guys talk business."

Tom stood up and turned to his ranch foreman. "You look serious, Jack. What is it?"

"Have you booked a honeymoon, Tom?"

From the look on Tom's face Jack knew he hadn't even given it a thought.

After checking on her sleeping baby, Elizabeth called Carol.

"Did you talk to Edith?" the bride-to-be asked.

"Yes, and your cake should be beautiful."

"Thank you so much." Carol hesitated, then added, "Elizabeth, I have one more favor to ask you."

"Anything. You name it."

"Will you be my matron of honor?"

Elizabeth was dumbfounded. She'd never been in anyone's wedding party. In fact, she'd never been to a wedding. Her own had been a quickie without a reception.

"Elizabeth," Carol prompted when she didn't reply. "I'd love for you to be my matron of honor."

"But I'll have the baby to take care of."

"We can get someone to take care of Jenny and Brady."

"But I don't have anything to wear."

"We'll get you a dress."

Elizabeth had run out of excuses. "Okay, Carol, I'll do it." A big grin lit up her face as she thought of the ceremony and the romance and the flowers and the cake. It was going to be a beautiful affair, and she was so honored that Carol had chosen her.

"Great," Carol said. "It's going to be perfect. Tom's asking Jack to be his best man. You two will make a lovely couple."

Elizabeth dropped the phone.

CHAPTER EIGHT

"Is something wrong?"

Elizabeth jumped. She hadn't heard Jack come into the kitchen. She picked up the phone, hung it up and turned to him.

"Nothing's wrong," she said quickly.

"Want to buy them a wedding present?"

"Oh! I'd forgotten about a present. I need to get a dress, too."

"For what?"

"Carol wants me to be her matron of honor. I need to buy a dress."

"Good. I need to buy a tux." He smiled at her, his blue eyes twinkling. "I'm the best man."

"You're going to *buy* a tux?"

"Aren't you going to buy a dress?"

"Well, yes. Will you have another opportunity to wear it?"

"Yeah, I'm planning on it."

"May I go with you and do my shopping, too?"

"Sure. I'm leaving just after lunch."

"Thank you, Jack."

"No problem."

She hurried upstairs.

Jack stood there, watching her departure. A smile played across his face. Yesterday she'd been jealous when she thought he had another girl. Today she was jittery at the thought of being partnered with him at Tom's wedding. He hadn't missed her dropping the phone and the splash of color on her cheeks when he came in.

It was going to be an interesting wedding.

But first he needed to buy a gift.

Earlier when he'd been talking to Tom, Tom mentioned getting some new furniture for their bedroom. He also wanted to spruce up the room with a more formal sitting area in front of the fireplace. That would make a perfect gift.

She had the money to buy her dress for the wedding. And he'd get to see her in it before anyone else. That thought made him smile to himself, his eyes dancing.

"I've been thinking about my gift to Tom and Carol and I had an idea for you, too."

Elizabeth turned to him as he drove them into town to shop. "What do you have in mind?"

He told her about the bedroom set he planned on buying. "I thought you might want to give them a TV so they could go to their room for some privacy in the evenings."

"You're right, Jack. I think that's a good idea, but I don't know anything about televisions. Can you help me pick out one?"

"Sure." After a moment he said, "Are you saying you didn't have a television?"

She shook her head.

"Did you not want one?"

"Reggie never saw a reason to buy one. I hadn't had one when we got married, so I guess he assumed I didn't want one."

"He wasn't much of a husband, was he? I mean, aside from the obvious, he didn't know you very well."

"Let's just say he didn't waste any effort trying to get to know me."

Because talking about Reggie seemed to sadden her, he changed the subject. "You know, this is the second time in a week that we've gone shopping. That's pretty amazing. I never shop that often."

"You could've fooled me."

He grinned. "I didn't think I knew what to do. The salesladies helped me a lot."

"Yes, I'm sure the salesladies helped you, but I think you did an amazing job."

"With no cooperation from you, by the way."

"That's true. I didn't think Tom should spend that much on us. I didn't feel he had a reason. After all, he didn't really know us."

"You were all he had left of his son."

"I wasn't sure he'd be glad to know he had anything left of Reggie."

"He didn't realize how bad Reggie had gotten. I was hearing things about Reggie, but Tom didn't hear. He thought his son wasn't good at letting his dad know how he was doing, but he forgave him for that."

He turned and looked at Elizabeth. "He still has a future in Brady and Jenny, thanks to you."

"I'm glad for him," Elizabeth said, "and I'm glad for Brady and Jenny. They now know their grandfather."

"And they're now going to have a grandmother, too."

"Did you know she'd miscarried twice? I felt so sorry for her when she told me that."

"Yeah, we knew that. I thought she seemed awfully lonesome."

"Now she'll have a lot of family."

"Except me. I'm not really family."

"But Tom said he regards you like his son. Only a nicer version."

"I appreciate Tom saying that, but I'm not like Reggie. And I have my own parents."

"You never talk about them. Are they local?"

Though he didn't want to talk about himself, he felt she at least deserved some details. After all, she'd divulged the truth about her addicted mother and unknown father.

"The family ranch is up near Tulsa. My mother passed away five years ago, but my dad's still alive. He's retired now. He turned over the ranch to my two older brothers." He tried to keep any emotion out of his voice.

Judging from the sympathetic look in her eyes, Elizabeth detected some. "Do you see them much?"

He shook his head and looked back to the road. "Every couple of years since I've been at Tom's." He should've just left it at that, but he added, "Not much for me there."

At her puzzled look he added, "My brothers got the ranch. There was nothing left for me."

"But you have family here, Jack. Don't you see that?" Her eyes pleaded with him to understand, but he only said, "Not anymore."

"So you're still thinking about leaving?" There was anxiety etched in her face. He knew she felt guilty about that.

"Yeah. I don't want to take care of the ranch until Brady is ready to take the reins."

"Will you go back home?"

"No." There was no chance of that.

"But can't you work out something until you find a better place?"

"I don't think I can find time to look for another ranch and still run this one."

"But you have a little time, don't you?" He thought her voice quavered.

"No, not really."

"But I don't think— I mean, can't you stay another year?"

"No. I don't want to go through spring roundup here."

"You plan to leave that soon?"

"Yeah."

Logically he knew that was the right thing to do. He had the desire and the means to buy his own ranch; it was always what he'd envisioned himself doing with his life. But emotionally he wasn't quite so sure. With Elizabeth and the kids there, the Ransom Ranch was going to be harder to put behind him.

Elizabeth turned forward in her seat, and they passed the rest of the ride in silence.

When they reached the mall, she opened her door, pulling her coat around her.

Jack got out and hurried around his truck to face her.

"Elizabeth, I'm not trying to be mean. But if I don't have a chance to buy the ranch, I need to move on."

Elizabeth pulled away from Jack's hold and walked toward the mall. She didn't want to walk beside him.

He didn't try to talk to her again.

When they went in the store they had shopped in last time, she went to the department for evening gowns. Jack followed her.

"Why are you coming here?" she asked.

"You said you wanted my help."

"No, I've changed my mind."

Despite that, he continued walking with her.

"I don't want you to come with me. Do you hear me?" When he didn't listen, she grabbed his arm. "I don't want your help. I want you to go do your own shopping."

"Give it up, Elizabeth. No matter what you say, I'm going with you."

She wanted to scream at him, but she wouldn't do that. She stepped into the department and looked for a saleslady. When one appeared, she explained that she was looking for a matron of honor gown.

The saleslady led her to a long rack of long gowns and party dresses and Elizabeth began flipping through them. The saleslady stepped back and asked Jack a question.

"What kind of dress does your wife like?"

"I don't know. I'm not her husband."

"Oh, I apologize. I just assumed since you were with her that you were her husband."

"No, she's a widow."

"Oh, my. Does she want to wear black?"

"No. She wants to honor the bride."

"Yes, of course."

"I think she'll need some advice, and she's not talking to me."

"I'll take care of it, sir." She stepped up to Elizabeth. "Can I offer you some assistance? There's one gown that I think you might like. Let me go get it."

She came back carrying a sapphire-blue gown with a high bodice and a flowing skirt. "That's gorgeous."

"The color matches your eyes."

Elizabeth stepped back from the rack. She couldn't imagine another gown that would be any better. "I'll try this one on."

"Certainly, ma'am. This way, please." The saleslady led the way to the fitting room.

Moments later when Elizabeth emerged in the blue gown, Jack was sitting in a chair, waiting for her. When he saw her, a feeling overcame him. A wish, really. He wished he was her husband.

He'd admired Elizabeth since he first saw her. She was beautiful. Though she was tired when she first arrived, she hadn't shrunk back from cooking and cleaning. Her generosity and her eagerness to please had impressed him.

She opened her heart to Tom, expecting nothing in return. For all he'd given her she'd been grateful, and she'd raised her son to be thankful, despite what little they'd had.

She was a remarkable woman.

If he had a choice, he'd like to stay at the Ransom Ranch. With her. If he thought he could have that ranch as his own, and Elizabeth as his wife, he'd be a happy man.

But that wasn't meant to be.

"This gown looks beautiful on you, Elizabeth. I think it's the one."

"Yes, I like it. I hope Carol does."

"I don't see how she could think otherwise." He smiled at her. "You know, I think I remember a little dress I bought Jenny that is almost that exact color."

"It's settled, then."

When she'd changed, they headed off to find Jack's tuxedo.

He, too, settled on the first one he tried on. Elizabeth thought he looked so distinguished in the black tux with a white shirt and black bowtie. And handsome. Very handsome.

Then again, she thought the same thing

when he came in dirty and dusty from a hard day on the ranch.

The tailor went right to work on the alterations, giving them two hours to find wedding presents.

In the furniture department Jack made his choices quickly. Elizabeth bought pillows, a comforter and sheets to go with Jack's gift.

"I thought Brady and Jenny could give them those presents," she explained.

"They'll get a lot of invitations to birthday parties if they give those kinds of gifts."

Elizabeth laughed. "How many times does one get a new grandparent?"

"Good point."

They went next to the electronics department to find a television. With his help she picked out the top of the line.

"Tom and Carol won't want you to spend this much," Jack cautioned her.

"Why won't he worry about how much you've spent?"

"He knows that I've saved my money."

"In order to buy his ranch."

"But he knows it's not for sale. He's made that clear."

"Maybe if I talked to him? Maybe I can convince him to sell the ranch to you, if he and Carol can continue to live there."

"I don't think that's possible."

"Why not?" She was searching for the elusive explanation that Jack failed to give.

"It doesn't matter. He wants to save the ranch for Brady."

"But I don't want Brady to grow up like his daddy."

"His daddy didn't do much on the ranch."

"Then maybe Brady should work on the ranch. To learn how to be a rancher, not just an owner."

"I understand that, but I won't be there to help him." There was a finality in his voice that Elizabeth hated hearing.

"I know," she said, unable to keep the sadness from her tone.

She went back to the televisions and paid for the one she chose. They had it sent to the loading dock.

"When are they delivering the furniture?"

"They promised to deliver it Friday at two."

"How will you keep it hidden from Tom?"

"I'm sending him up to my room to get peace and quiet for his nap."

"That's nice. Won't he be suspicious?"

"No. He'll believe me."

"Of course he will," Elizabeth said with sorrow as she thought about how much Tom would miss having Jack around.

And so would she.

* * *

Elizabeth and Jack walked into a happy family scene. Tom and Brady were playing cards and Carol was cuddling Jenny. A fire was burning in the fireplace and there was a heavenly scent coming from the kitchen.

"Carol, you fixed dinner! It smells great," Elizabeth exclaimed.

"Shopping always makes me tired and I thought it might have the same effect on you," Carol said.

"Yes, it does," Elizabeth said as she shot Jack a dirty look.

Carol looked at Elizabeth then back at Jack. "Did you two have an argument?"

Elizabeth straightened and wiped all emotion from her face. "No, of course not. We just…disagreed."

Jack sighed before saying, "We'll talk about it later, Elizabeth."

"Maybe if we eat, everyone will feel better," Tom suggested.

"I feel fine," Brady pronounced.

"Yeah, but I think you'll want some of that banana pudding Carol made."

"Yeah!"

Smiling, Elizabeth ruffled her son's hair. "How's Jenny?"

"Oh, she's just the sweetest thing," Carol cooed as she talked to the baby. "She has the biggest blue eyes for such a little thing."

"Just like her mother," Jack pointed out.

Carol didn't notice any disagreement then. "Yes, just like her mother," she agreed.

Tom began stacking the cards, saying, "We'd better get these cards put away, Brady, so Grandma can serve us dinner."

Brady looked up at Carol. "'Grandma'? Are you going to be my grandma?"

Carol beamed at the little boy. "Yes, if you don't mind, I'd like to be your grandma."

"Okay."

"Come on, Brady," Jack said. "I'll help you clean up. Maybe we can wash our hands together."

"I'll come, too," Tom said following them.

Elizabeth stared at them wondering why all three of the "men" were going into the downstairs bathroom.

"What's wrong with Elizabeth?"

Before Jack answered Tom he shot a look at Brady. He wasn't sure they should be talking in front of the boy. "Um, we got into a discussion about the, uh, wedding."

"Does Mommy not want to go?" Brady asked, reminding Jack that he was right to worry. He came up with some story to satisfy the child.

"Sure she does. But she wanted pink roses on the cake and I wanted red roses."

"So who won?" Brady was certainly amused by the contest.

"I guess she did because we're having pink roses," Jack answered.

"Do they taste good?" Brady asked.

"I think so. Go ask your mom, if your hands are clean."

After Brady scurried out, Tom asked, "What is Elizabeth really upset about?"

"What you and I discussed the other night."

Tom frowned and shook his head. "I wish I could change my mind, Jack, but I want the ranch for Brady."

"It's okay, Tom. I understand. I just thought when you get back from your honeymoon I should start looking for a new ranch."

Tom gripped Jack's shoulder in a large

rugged hand. "It seems a poor way to pay you for your loyalty."

"You've paid me a good salary, Tom, and I've been happy here. But change is good for all of us."

"I won't argue that, because I wouldn't want the kids or Elizabeth to go. I'm feeling better now and I want to help out around the ranch, but I don't think I can run it."

"We'll find someone for you before I leave. Just enjoy your honeymoon."

"Thanks, Jack." Tom started to leave and then turned and looked Jack in the eye. "You know, you could just marry Elizabeth."

CHAPTER NINE

JACK thought a lot about what Tom had said. He'd realized Elizabeth had only been widowed a short while, but according to Elizabeth, Reggie had seen little of her since Jenny had been conceived.

That thought occupied his mind through the rest of the week and throughout the wedding ceremony. As he listened to Tom's vows to Carol, he imagined taking the same step with Elizabeth. She looked beautiful in her blue gown, just as little Jenny did. Elizabeth carried Jenny in her arms, with the baby scarcely aware of what was going on around her.

At the reception, held at a venue in town, Elizabeth was still a little shy around the women she'd met this week. It seemed natural to put an arm around her for reassurance. At least, that's what Jack told himself. Then he picked Brady up in his arms, and Jack really began to feel like this was his little family.

"They aren't coming back to the house, are they?" Elizabeth asked. "I didn't get the bed made."

"I think they're heading straight for the airport. Do you want me to go ask them?"

She shook her head. "I guess it doesn't matter. You already hung the television over the fireplace. Maybe I should take the kids and run home and fix up the linens."

"Let me go talk to Tom. Then we can make a decision."

"*We?*"

"I just meant we should figure out if they're

going back to the house. If not, we need to stay here and wish them well."

"I guess you're right. But Brady and I, with Jenny, could go on—"

"And drive my truck?"

"I thought maybe you could get a ride with someone," she said.

"I don't think I want to stand out on the street corner with my thumb in the air."

She hadn't meant to offend him. "You're right. I shouldn't have mentioned it."

"I'm only kidding. You can have the truck if that's what you want."

"Maybe I can use Carol's car."

"Let me go ask Tom what their plan is. I'll be right back. Don't move." Jack hurried across the floor to grab Tom's arm to ask him their plans.

Tom looked surprised. "We're going to go grab our bags. We left them both at the house."

"Okay. Elizabeth and I are going to run

ahead, then, to get something ready and then we'll see you there."

"Wait! What do you need to get ready?"

"Your presents from us. We want you to see them before you go."

"You got us presents?"

"Tom, everyone gets presents when they get married."

"Elizabeth got us a present, too?"

"Yes, and so did Brady and Jenny."

"But we—"

Jack held up a hand to stop him. "Tom, we have to congratulate you. Not everyone gets a second chance." He grinned at his friend. "You old dog."

Tom hesitated before saying, "I hope Elizabeth gets one."

"You just make sure Carol has a good time. We'll talk when you get back."

Jack went back to Elizabeth and explained.

She gathered their coats. "I think we need to take the cake. Carol said we needed to take home whatever was left of it. Oh, and the gifts, too."

"Okay. Brady, you come help me."

"Me?" Brady asked, surprised.

"You bet, son. We men are the lifters."

Brady beamed up at his mother. "We men are the lifters, Mommy."

His mother answered with a touch of sarcasm in her voice. "Yes, I heard that, too."

Brady grabbed Jack's hand, ready to go.

"We'll be back in a few minutes," Jack said as they headed off for their manly duty.

Elizabeth stared after Jack, wondering what he was up to. It seemed to her that he had other things going on than just a wedding. She wanted Brady to have a good role model, and his grandfather might be too old, but she couldn't count on Jack to be around. She wished she could talk him into staying, but he seemed determined to move on.

She pulled her mind together to focus on what she would need to do when she reached the house. The freshly laundered sheets needed to be put on the bed, with the coverlet and pillows. She also needed to put out a centerpiece she'd purchased for the coffee table in the sitting area. It was the perfect finishing touch for the bedroom.

"But first I'll have to tuck you in, sweetie, so I'll have both arms," Elizabeth cooed to Jenny. She leaned down and kissed her baby's cheek. Brady was a terrific son, and her baby girl was extrasweet. These were the two best presents anyone had ever given her.

Jack came in the door, with Brady. "We'll get the cake and then we're ready. Why don't you get the baby in the truck?"

She did as Jack suggested. Moments later her son ran to the truck ahead of him.

"Mommy, Grandpa's going to come home!"

"I know, sweetheart."

"Will he come back again?" Brady asked.

"Of course he will."

"Daddy never did."

"Sweetheart, your daddy never planned on coming home. He had other things going on."

Jack stepped beside the boy. "We're not like your daddy, Brady. We believe in coming home every night. Your grandpa will be home as soon as he and Carol see Paris."

"Really?"

"I guarantee it."

The ride back to the ranch was peppered with more of Brady's questions and observations about the wedding. When the truck pulled up to the house, Brady attempted to jump out over his mother.

"Wait a minute, Brady. I'll help you," Jack called. "Don't mess up your clothes."

As he was talking to Brady, he reached in to help Elizabeth out. "Go tuck in little Jenny and I'll meet you in the bedroom."

She immediately said, "You mean Tom's bedroom."

"Of course, I meant Tom's bedroom."

She gave a nod and walked upstairs, cuddling the baby.

Once Jenny was tucked in, Elizabeth went downstairs to make up Tom and Carol's new bed. As she worked, she couldn't help thinking how much she'd hoped it would work out for her here. That Tom could keep the ranch prosperous and the children could stay with their grandparents. But now she doubted that outcome. Without Jack, how could Tom keep the ranch?

She put on the shams just as Jack came in.

"Just in time. That looks beautiful, Elizabeth."

"I don't need any help," she snapped when she saw it was Jack.

"Now don't be grumpy. I want to help."

"Well, I don't want your help."

"Elizabeth, what's going on? Are you mad at me?"

His question brought her to her senses. She couldn't blame Jack for his dreams. "No, I just—I had hoped— Oh, never mind. When Tom proposed to Carol, I'd hoped we'd have a family here, but that's not happening. I don't know if they'll survive or whether we'll actually be able to stay. Tom can't run the ranch."

"I think you, Brady and Jenny have a great future here."

"Doing what? Raising cows? What do I know about that?"

He smiled at her. "I have a plan, so quit worrying."

"What are you talking about?" she asked skeptically.

"Don't you have any faith in me, Elizabeth?"

She turned away from him. "I don't see why I should." After a moment she began walking to the kitchen. Jack followed her as she spoke. "Why don't you and Brady come have some cake? It will take his mind off what's happening."

"I don't think anything tragic is happening."

"Just eat some cake."

"Brady," Jack called.

"Yes, Jack?" the little boy said as he came running.

"Let's have some cake. Your mom's afraid we're going to be hungry."

The boy grinned. "I like cake."

"Okay," Jack said as he sliced them each a piece. "Have a seat at the table."

Before he put two slices on the table he turned to Elizabeth.

"Just one more thing."

"Yes?" she asked.

Jack leaned over and kissed her.

"You kissed my mommy!"

Jack had been staring into space reliving the kiss when Brady interrupted him a while later. "Yeah, I did. Don't you kiss your mommy?"

"Not on her mouth."

"Well, you're not supposed to kiss her on the mouth, but I am."

"Why?"

"Because your mommy and I, uh, like each other." Jack wasn't sure Elizabeth would accept that explanation, but he did. He'd been thinking about tasting those lips for a while now.

He wondered what Elizabeth thought. At first

she'd simply stood there, staring at him with her big blue eyes. Then she skedaddled upstairs, claiming she needed to check on the baby.

"Does Mommy like it?" Brady asked.

"I don't know, Brady. I hope so." Just as he opened his mouth to add to the explanation, he heard a car in the driveway.

"Hey, I think Tom and Carol are here. Go up and get your mom and tell her they're here." He hoped Elizabeth's sensibilities would be soothed with Tom and Carol's arrival.

Brady jumped up to go get his mother. Climbing the stairs, he shouted to his mom like all kids do. "Mommy! They're here! They're here!"

Jack moved to the door to open it wide for the newlyweds.

* * *

Elizabeth didn't want to go downstairs, but she couldn't let Tom and Carol know there was a problem. She gathered Jenny in her arms, hoping she'd provide a defense against Jack.

Not that she necessarily wanted a defense.

She had to admit that Jack's kiss packed a wallop. Just a light touching of his lips to hers had the electric current of a power plant. What would a real kiss be like?

She refused to think of it.

At Brady's urging, she came to the edge of the stairs. Taking that first step was the hardest, but she wanted to do this right.

She reached the bottom of the stairs with her children around providing protection from Jack. They greeted Tom and Carol. Maintaining her distance from Jack, she opened the door to their bedroom. "We hope you like it," she said.

They admired the furniture, the television,

the fire in the fireplace, but most of all, they loved the new bed.

"It's so big," Carol said.

Tom agreed. "It looks wonderful."

"We're glad you like it," Jack said.

"Jenny and Brady gave you the linens," Elizabeth pointed out.

"They're lovely." Carol bent down to hug the little boy.

He stood proudly. "I helped Mommy."

"Yes, you did, and you and Jenny are special children," Carol responded.

"Of course they are," Tom added. "They're *our* grandchildren."

Carol's eyes glistened with tears. "Oh, Tom, that's so sweet of you to say that."

"I think we lost them," Jack said jokingly as Tom and Carol gazed into each other's eyes.

"Don't tease them," Elizabeth said sharply.

"I think they'd better get to the airport quickly if they're going to have a honeymoon in Paris."

"I think you're right," Tom said. "Where are our bags?"

"They're both sitting over here. I'll carry them out to the car for you," Jack said.

Jack took the bags out to the car, while Elizabeth and the children shrugged on coats and followed out to the porch. After last goodbye hugs, the newlyweds were on their way, waving as their car went down the drive.

Behind her Elizabeth felt Jack step close and put a hand on her shoulder. "What are you doing?" she gasped.

"Presenting a picture of our family."

"What are you talking about?"

"Showing Tom what he wants to see."

"I still don't know what you're talking about."

"Tom thinks of us as his family, that's all."

"I don't see how he can think that since you're leaving."

"Go on inside where it's warm and I'll tell you," Jack ordered.

Elizabeth went inside, but she wasn't sure Jack was going to tell her what she wanted to hear. It was time for Jenny's bottle, so she prepared it.

Brady had come in with her and sat down at his partially eaten cake. She wasn't surprised when Jack joined them. She thought about suggesting that he eat separately from them, but she didn't think he'd agree to that.

"You see, Elizabeth, Tom expects us to maintain his home while he's gone. My particular job is to make sure that you and Brady and Jenny are taken care of."

"I can take care of us," Elizabeth insisted.

"Is that so? I'll be the one taking care of you and the kids. It's my job."

"Somehow, I think I'll be taking care of you unless you want to starve to death and wear dirty clothes."

"Okay, so we'll take care of each other. Tom likes the idea of having a family again and I'm going to make sure he comes home to a family. Brady, will you be glad when Grandpa comes back?"

"Are you sure he's coming back?" Brady asked.

"I told you he was, son."

"Don't call him that," Elizabeth exclaimed.

Jack looked up at her, confused. "What?"

"Never mind. Brady, go hang your coat up."

As Brady did as he was told, Jack leaned in real close to her. "You've got to relax, Elizabeth. Things are different now."

Elizabeth prepared a simple meal that night, knowing Brady and Jack had filled up at the wedding reception. When she called them to the table, Jack and Brady came downstairs together.

"Brady, did you put away your toys?" Elizabeth asked.

"Sure, Mommy. Jack helped me."

"I hope you told him thank you."

"I did," Brady said agreeably.

"He was great, Elizabeth," Jack said. "He thanked me and showed me the right place to put things. He keeps his room neat, too. He's a great kid."

Elizabeth turned her back on Jack. She didn't want him to praise her children.

Jack opened the silverware drawer and took out what they needed for the meal.

Elizabeth stopped him. "I'll do that."

"No need. I can help."

She put out the cold-cut platter and said, "Brady, I found the little oranges you like."

Brady climbed up to the table, anxious to see his mother's surprise. "Thanks, Mom!"

"We bought those when I was trying to tempt Tom to eat something different," Jack said. "Thank goodness we found Carol instead. She'll do a better job."

"Yes, I imagine she will. Tom is a lucky man."

"Yeah, I kind of think you're right. She'll keep Tom in line."

"She will and he'll be able to take care of her. That's the way a marriage should work."

"I'm glad you mentioned that," Jack replied.

Elizabeth's mouth instantly dried up. "What do you mean?"

"I don't think I should tell you yet."

"Tell me what?"

"I think you'll understand it well enough."

"Does Tom know?" she asked.

"It was his suggestion."

"Unless you're going to tell me what you're talking about, just be quiet and eat. Brady's almost asleep."

Brady opened his eyes wide. "No I'm not, Mommy," he protested.

She leaned over and kissed his forehead. "Yes, you are, sweetie, and you'll need to go to bed as soon as you finish eating dinner."

Brady sank back into his chair. "Okay, Mommy."

Jack asked, "If I promise to go to bed, will you give me a kiss too?"

She froze and then glared at him. "You've had enough kisses today."

He smiled a broad smile and his eyes twinkled. "I think everyone needs kisses. I'll be glad to supply you, Brady and Jenny with kisses."

"I can take care of Brady and Jenny. They don't need your kisses."

"But what about you? Don't you need my kisses?"

"I most certainly do not," Elizabeth protested.

"Oh, I think you're wrong," Jack said as he leaned in and kissed her again.

CHAPTER TEN

ELIZABETH helped Brady spread red and white icing on a candy cane cookie a few afternoons later when Jack came in from the ranch.

"You're back early," she said without looking up.

"It's turned awfully cold. I need to warm up."

She had her suspicions and looked at him skeptically. Whichever, she cautioned herself to keep her distance.

The second cookie sheet was ready to come out of the oven when Jack joined them.

"What are you doing?" he asked.

"That should be obvious, Jack," Elizabeth said.

Brady immediately piped up. "We're making Christmas cookies for Santa."

"You are? Do I get one?"

Brady giggled. "You're not Santa!"

"No, but I've been friends with him a long time."

"You have?" the little boy asked in amazement.

"Yeah, he and I are old friends."

"Jack, you're misleading Brady."

"Elizabeth, Brady should know that Santa needs help occasionally. He might need help getting Brady's toys to him."

"Do you want a cookie?" Elizabeth asked.

"Sure. Warm cookies on a cold afternoon are the best."

She took the cookies off the cookie sheet. "These will have to cool. You may choose one cookie each and then you may choose another one after we've decorated them."

"Hey, that's better than I thought," Jack said.

With Elizabeth's willing volunteers, she began mixing up more colors for the other cookies. She hadn't expected to share this moment with Jack, but she supposed he deserved it. He'd been good while Tom and Carol had been gone. Most of the time anyway.

The monitor blared just then with Jenny's cries. Elizabeth started to go get her, but Jack stopped her with a hand on her arm.

"Let me go get her," Jack offered.

"But she'll need her diaper changed."

"I can do that."

When Jack came downstairs a few minutes later with a happy Jenny in his arms, Elizabeth decided he'd done a good job.

"Thank you, Jack," she said. "Brady and I

got two cookie sheets ready and in the oven in the meantime."

Jack grinned. "And Jenny didn't even complain."

"Her bottle will be ready in just a minute, if you can hold her," Elizabeth said.

"Of course I can. Jenny and I are friends. Would you like me to feed her?"

Elizabeth stopped short. "Why should you feed my baby?"

"Because I'm going to be her— Her friend."

Jack sure was acting strange today, Elizabeth thought. "Aren't you going back out?"

"No, I think I'll stay in the rest of the day. The cold is bitter and the kitchen is warm. You and Brady can decorate cookies and I'll feed Jenny."

Elizabeth hesitated, but she wanted the experience to be good for Brady, so she agreed.

By the end of the afternoon Brady had made

a plateful of unusually decorated cookies. But he thought they were terrific and that was good enough for her. He even took one of them to feed to Jack.

Jack seemed to enjoy the family scene too, which surprised Elizabeth. In fact, she had such a good time she didn't realize it was past time to make dinner. She hurriedly cleaned up.

"Elizabeth, why don't we go to a restaurant?" Jack offered. "You've been working all day."

"Jack, that's ridiculous. It's my job."

"I'd like some good Mexican food to warm me up. How about you, Brady? Would you like some Mexican food?"

"What's that?"

"It's food that they serve at José's Bar & Grill in town. It's really good. Want to go?"

"Jack, you go. It's too hard for Brady, Jenny and me."

"No, I refuse to go without you. Just grab your coats and I'll take care of everything."

Fifteen minutes later they entered the restaurant, warm and redolent with Mexican spices. Jack settled Jenny's car seat on an upturned chair and helped Elizabeth off with her coat. "We never did get you a new coat."

"I'm sure it's not worth an hour-long drive to Oklahoma City."

"Well, we do have one store that has coats, but it's kind of a Western store. I don't know if you'll find what you want."

"We'll see."

"Hey, Jack," a voice called from across the restaurant.

"Hey, Bill," Jack answered. "Come on over and I'll introduce you. Elizabeth, this is Bill 'José' Metcalf. He's the owner of this place."

"Hello, Mr. Metcalf. Do I call you Bill or José?"

"Anything you want, darlin'."

Jack's arm came around Elizabeth. "Hands off, pal. This is Reggie's widow."

Elizabeth was startled by Jack's behavior. "Jack, you shouldn't—I mean, I'm very glad to meet you, Bill."

Elizabeth met several more people through Jack, and it was a a fun evening away from her responsibilities. Brady loved the Mexican food, especially the chips and queso. In fact he ate so much he fell asleep before it was time to leave.

"It's a good thing I'm with you," Jack said. "Otherwise you'd be hard put to get both kids home."

"I can carry them."

"Not together you can't. I'll take Brady, you take Jenny."

"But we have to pay."

"I'll take care of it. Just a second."

"No, you can't pay for us," Elizabeth protested.

"Honey, it's too late."

Before she could ask what he meant, Jack got up. She'd hoped to come again, but not if he was going to insist on paying. Then again, he'd be leaving soon.

Once they were in the truck driving home, both children asleep, Jack asked, "What did you think of José's?"

"I liked it."

"Good, we can go eat there again."

"We?"

"Yeah. Why not?" Jack asked.

"Because I think you'll be gone."

"Did you know José's does Christmas dinner for a lot of people?"

"You think I'm going to eat Christmas dinner at José's?"

"No, I thought you might volunteer."

"Volunteer for what?"

"He feeds a lot of people who otherwise couldn't afford it or who don't have a place to go for Christmas. A lot of us have gotten together to help him. It's a nice thing for Christmas."

Elizabeth didn't hesitate. "Yes, I'd be willing to help out if you're sure they'll welcome me to the group. It will be a nice way to say thank you for all the blessings I've received."

"Good. I'll let them know. You realize it's hard work, don't you?"

"Yes, but I can do hard work."

"It will be a good way to get to know everyone."

"Yes, I'm sure you're right."

They rode in silence for several minutes. Then Jack asked a question he'd wanted to know the answer to. "Did Reggie come to see you after you found out you were pregnant?"

"With Jenny? No. When I told him I was pregnant, he was furious. He accused me of taking a lover."

"That must have been difficult."

"Yes." She didn't add anything else. The emotions she'd felt at his response to her pregnancy had destroyed any hope of a marriage between them. Still, she'd held on to hope until Jenny was born. By then, it had been too late.

"Did you ever discuss Jenny's birth with him after that?"

"No, he didn't want to listen."

"I'm glad Jenny doesn't have to know that."

"I certainly don't intend to tell her."

"Me, neither."

When he turned the truck into the driveway, Elizabeth glanced ahead at the house. It was brightly lit. But how? She was sure they'd carefully locked up before they'd left. "Jack, did we leave that many lights on when we left?"

He focused on the house. "No, we didn't."

"Who could it be? Tom and Carol aren't due back for another five days!"

"I guess we'll find out." He turned to her. "Stay here with the doors locked while I check out the house."

She didn't argue, but she stared after him, praying for his safety.

"Mommy?"

"Oh, Brady. I didn't know you were awake."

"Why aren't we getting out?"

"Jack is checking out the house. Some lights were turned on that we thought we'd turned off."

"Do you think someone is stealing our presents?" Brady asked, his eyes big.

"I don't know, sweetie."

Just then Jack came out on the porch and reached for Elizabeth's door. "We have a surprise. Come on in."

When he realized Brady was awake, he reached out for the boy. "Come on, little guy. I think you'll like this surprise."

That unleashed Brady's many questions. Elizabeth smiled as she gathered up Jenny and climbed out of the truck.

When she opened the door to the house, she knew at once who had lit up the house. They'd left their suitcases in plain sight. "Brady, you're going to like this surprise."

"How do you know, Mommy?"

"I just think you'll like it," she said with a smile.

Then the bedroom door opened and Tom stepped out.

"Grandpa! You came back!" Brady exclaimed and launched himself to Tom's open arms.

"Of course I did, boy. Didn't you expect me?"

"I don't know. You were gone a long time."

"That's what I told Carol."

"Didn't she mind?" Elizabeth asked.

"No, she was ready to come back. She said she was ready to begin her new life as lady of the manor!"

"Tom Ransom, you make it sound like I'll be a lady of leisure!" Carol protested as she came out of the bedroom.

"Hello, Carol, and welcome home. We've missed you." Elizabeth smiled and held her arms for a hug. "How was Paris?"

"It had lots of museums and places to visit. And the food was good, but we got hungry for our kind of food. It was time to come home."

"We're glad you came back," Elizabeth said. "I'll pull together a meal."

"Leftovers will be fine, Elizabeth," Carol said.

"That's just it. We ate out this evening. How about hamburgers? That shouldn't take long."

"Perfect! That's what we were thinking of. Are you sure you don't mind?"

"Not at all." She set Jenny down and took off her coat. Jack came over and lifted Jenny into his lap.

"Don't wake her," Elizabeth said.

"I won't. I just thought she'd be more comfortable if I held her." While he was giving his excuse, he was gently rocking Jenny in his arms.

"Likely excuse!" Carol teased.

"You can see through it, can you?" Jack asked, grinning.

"Yes, because I wanted to do the same," Carol admitted.

"Okay, I'll let you hold her since you've been gone for a few days."

"Bless you, Jack! That's so nice of you."

When Tom came into the kitchen, he found his wife contentedly rocking Jenny. "How did you get that job?"

Carol smiled at him. "Jack volunteered me for it…because he realized I'd missed her."

"Good for Jack. I swear she would've traded me for Jenny several times," Tom growled.

Elizabeth smiled at Tom. "It's a deep-seated urge, the need to have children. Jenny is honored to help Carol."

"Thank you, Elizabeth," Tom said.

"Hey, I'm the one who gave up Jenny to Carol. I should get some credit."

"That's true, Jack." Elizabeth smiled at him. "Perhaps I'll let you help with the dishes."

"Thanks a lot," Jack said, taking the teasing good-naturedly.

When the burgers were ready, Carol handed Jack the baby and they sat down.

"Grandpa, did you bring me a present?"

Elizabeth jerked her head around. "Brady, what did you say?"

"A boy in Sunday school class said my

grandpa would bring me a present from Paris…whatever that is."

"You do not ask for presents, Brady."

Tom tried to answer, determined to rescue Brady. But Elizabeth would have none of it. "It's time for you to go to bed, Brady," she said sternly.

"Yes, ma'am, Mommy. I'm sorry I got in trouble."

"I know, sweetie. I'll be up in a minute to see you."

"I'll come help you get ready, Brady," Jack said.

The little boy extended his hand to the big man and they went up the stairs together.

"He's a good man, Elizabeth."

"Yes, he is, and he'll make some woman a great husband."

"But not you?"

"No, Tom, not me."

"Why? Did you love Reggie that much?"

Elizabeth bowed her head. After a moment she said, "No, Tom, unfortunately, I didn't, but by the time I realized it, it was too late. I already had Brady. I decided to make the best of it, but then Reggie came back and—and we created Jenny."

"Surely you don't regret Jenny?" Carol asked.

"No! Never! But I don't want to risk marriage again, when my judgment is so awful."

Tom laid a comforting hand on her shoulder. "Honey, you can blame Reggie for that. He learned to play the role that people wanted to see. You're not the first one he misled."

"But I don't want to run that risk."

Tom sat back. "Then I guess I can't sell the ranch to Jack.

"My only hope was that you and Jack might marry. I know he'd treat Brady as his own son."

"Tom, I can't— I'm not suited to marriage." She stood and ran up the stairs.

Carol turned to her new husband. "Tom, I don't think you should've pushed her so. It's clear that she doesn't intend to marry again."

"But would that be fair? To let a woman that is genuine and loving lock herself in a deep freeze? I don't think that's fair, not when it's Reggie's fault. How can I live with that? She's perfect for Jack and I know he'll be good for her."

Carol reached out and patted his hand. "I know, dear. But I don't think you should put pressure on Elizabeth."

"Now, Carol, you don't bother your pretty little head with this. Jack and I will work it out."

She withdrew her hand from his. "I don't think I like your attitude, Tom."

"Carol, this is something Jack and I will discuss. It has nothing to do with you."

"Am I your wife, Tom? Were we standing in front of our minister, swearing to share our lives, to love and honor each other? Because that's what I remember!"

"Well, of course, honey. I promised to take care of you."

"That's not all I promised. Nor you."

She stood and moved to her suitcase. "I'll sleep upstairs if you don't mind."

"Carol, you come back here right now!"

"No, I won't." She stomped up the stairs.

"What's going on down here?" Jack asked as he came down the stairs.

"Carol and I had a…a little disagreement."

"It sounded more like a major disagreement. What's wrong?"

"No! I…I didn't want her to get upset. So I told her nor to worry about it. Everything would be fine."

"What was she worried about?"

"I had a discussion with Elizabeth about marrying again. She doesn't intend to. I tried to talk her into marriage but she wasn't having any of it. I tried to explain that I wanted her to live a full life, not rejecting love and marriage. But Carol said she didn't think I should press Elizabeth anymore. I told her not to worry about it."

"That didn't work?"

"No, she said we were supposed to share our lives." He hung his head. "She's going to sleep upstairs."

"I'm sure she'll rethink her choice in the morning. She loves you very much."

"I hope so."

When Tom went to his bedroom, Jack stood there with his hands on his hips. After thinking for several minutes, he turned and slowly climbed the stairs. He knocked on the door to Jenny's room. He could hear whispers inside and assumed that was where Carol had taken refuge.

Elizabeth opened the door. "Yes?"

"I want to talk to Carol."

"Carol, do you want to talk to Jack?"

"What does he have to say?"

Elizabeth turned back to Jack.

"I wanted her to know that Tom is very sad that she's not joining him in bed tonight."

"Is he apologizing?"

"No, Carol, but he was only trying to protect you."

"Carol, did you fight over me?" Elizabeth demanded.

"Yes, we did, and do you know what he told me? He told me not to concern myself with it."

"But, Carol—" Elizabeth began.

"You know better, Elizabeth. A marriage is either a marriage or it's a sham. I won't be involved in a sham."

Elizabeth lowered her head and took a minute before she looked at Jack. "I'm sorry, Jack, but I can't argue with that."

Then she closed the door in his face.

The Ransom household was at war.

CHAPTER ELEVEN

To Jack's surprise, Elizabeth had his breakfast ready when he came down the stairs the
next morning. Her back was to him as she
stood at the kitchen window looking out on a
bleak December morning.

"I didn't know you'd be up for breakfast."

She didn't bother turning around. "Of
course. It's my job."

"Aren't you going to eat with me?"

"No, I'll eat when Brady does."

"I kind of miss you at the table while I'm
eating. Why don't you fix a cup of coffee and
sit down?"

She turned then but busied herself at the sink. "I have some chores that need to be done. I'm trying to get some things done before Christmas."

"Do you need to go shopping again? I can take some time off and drive to Oklahoma City if you—"

"No, thank you. Carol offered to take me shopping so I won't have to interrupt your work."

"What does Brady want for Christmas?"

She shrugged. "I don't know exactly."

"I know something he's wanted for a long time."

She knew he was trying to engage her in conversation so she'd stay in the kitchen, but she couldn't resist hearing what he had to say. "What do you think he wants?"

"A puppy."

"I don't know how to train a puppy. That takes a lot of time and work."

"I can do it," Jack said.

She finally looked at him. Stared at him, actually. How could he do that when he was leaving in a few months? "That job needs more commitment than you can give," she snapped. Then she took off her apron and started up the stairs.

"Elizabeth, it's possible I won't be leaving the ranch."

She turned and came back down the few steps she had ascended, her heart pounding. "Are you serious?"

"Yeah, I'm serious. I'm considering my options."

"If I can help you in any way, please let me know."

Jack smiled. "I'll do that. Now, how about

that puppy for Brady? He wants one badly, and he can learn responsibility."

"I don't know if I—"

"Look, if you give him a puppy, I'll help him with it. I had a dog when I was young, too."

"But how will I know if you're really going to stay? If I got him a puppy and you left, I'd be in trouble."

"I promise I'll teach you and Brady everything you need to know before I leave, if I do."

"All right. Who do I talk to about a puppy?"

Jack smiled. "Well, the owner is difficult, but he has a soft spot for little boys."

"Do you think he'll sell me one?"

"Yeah, if you're willing to pay the price."

"How much is he asking?"

"I think a kiss should do it."

Elizabeth was confused. "That can't be right. I mean, I don't go around kissing strange men."

"And I don't want you to, either." Jack looked at her, a twinkle in his eye. "But I'm not exactly a stranger."

"What are you saying, Jack?"

"It's me, Elizabeth. I'm the owner."

Elizabeth stared at him, not finding the humor in Jack's little joke. "You were teasing me, weren't you?"

"I wasn't teasing you about staying. And I wasn't teasing you about the dog. I just wasn't forthcoming about *owning* the dog."

"Now I don't know what to believe!" She turned to run up the stairs.

"Elizabeth! The puppy is yours if you want it. Just say the word."

"I'll think about it." And she vanished upstairs.

Jack sighed as he watched her go. He never should have teased her about kissing him to pay for the dog. But he wasn't sure how she'd react to another kiss if he did it just because he wanted to kiss her.

After two kisses, he had to admit kissing Elizabeth had become an addiction.

But he couldn't spoil Brady's Christmas. He knew the boy was hoping to find his favorite dog under the Christmas tree. Jack remembered what it was like to want something so badly for Christmas.

Like he wanted Elizabeth.

"Brady, have you decided what to ask Santa for Christmas?"

She knew Jack was right that morning, and he'd jump up and down and scream for a puppy. But she had to be sure.

She was surprised to see a reluctance on his face.

After a hesitation, Brady, with an almost fearful look, said, "Yes, Mommy."

"What do you want?"

"Santa can bring anything, right?"

Elizabeth looked at Carol, eating her breakfast without her husband. "Well, within reason, sweetie. I know he'll try very hard to bring you what you want."

"Then I want a puppy…and a daddy."

Carol, as well as Elizabeth, stared at him.

"I know Grandpa chose you, Grandma, but I don't see why Santa can't bring Mommy a husband, a good one this time, not like Daddy."

Elizabeth stared at her son, unable to speak.

Carol, after noting Elizabeth's stunned expression, said, "Santa doesn't bring husbands or wives, Brady."

"Why not?"

Elizabeth finally pulled herself together. "Whatever made you ask for such a thing, Brady?"

"When we went to church, the other boys had daddies. They came to pick up their sons. I know Daddy didn't ever come to see me, so I figured it was me, but Jack said there was nothing wrong with me. He said he'd want me for his boy. And I thought Santa could make it happen."

"No, there's nothing wrong with you, Brady," Elizabeth assured him, hugging him, wishing she could provide him with a father who would love him as much as he deserved. "Jack was right. You'd be a great son for any man."

"So do you think you can marry Jack? I heard him and Grandpa talking about him staying here forever. I'd like that."

Elizabeth blinked rapidly to dispel her tears. She'd tried so hard to protect her son from his father. But it appeared nothing but the truth would do.

"Elizabeth, can I talk to you a second?" Carol said suddenly.

"Yes, of course." She moved to the sink where Carol stood.

"What is it?"

In a whisper, Carol said, "That's what Tom was talking about."

"What?"

"Tom was talking about you marrying Jack. They both think that would make it possible for Tom to sell the ranch to Jack because he would take care of the children."

"Surely that wouldn't be Jack's choice? I mean, he doesn't want to marry me. He hasn't said anything about that."

"I'm telling you that's what they were discussing last night."

After a moment of stunned silence, Elizabeth drew off her apron. "Can you listen for Jenny while I go to the barn?"

Carol nodded. "Take your time. You know I'm hoping she'll wake up while you're gone."

"I know," Elizabeth said with a smile.

Before she could leave the house, Brady asked, in a quiet voice, "Mommy, you aren't mad, are you?"

"No, sweetheart. And I'm not promising anything, but I'm going to see what I can do about your request."

"So Jack can be my daddy?"

She didn't know what to answer.

Elizabeth approached the barn, debating her impulsive decision to talk to Jack. It could be that she'd misread Jack's hints. He might not be interested in a marriage of convenience.

How embarrassing!

But she wasn't going to miss the opportunity to solve all her problems. She and Jack could pretend to be happily married and Brady could have a daddy. She just had to explain everything to Jack.

She opened the barn door, as if she was sneaking in.

But the creaking of the door eliminated her stealth.

"Who is it?"

He was here. She'd wondered if he might be out with the cowboys. Maybe she should say hoped. Then she wouldn't have to discuss the situation.

"It's Elizabeth," she called softly.

"Is something wrong?" Jack demanded, moving into the center aisle from one of the stalls at the far end.

"No! No, everything is fine. I just…just wanted to talk to you."

"Sure. I'll be in the house in about half an hour."

"Uh, no. I need to talk to you now." Elizabeth was getting cold feet, now that she was facing Jack, looking into his blue eyes.

"You don't want our conversation overheard? Is that the problem?"

"Y-yes."

"Okay. What's up?"

"Nothing! I mean—I had a strange feeling that you haven't been honest with me."

Jack stood up straight and took a long look at her. "About what?"

"About how you were going to stay here."

"Well, now, Elizabeth, I didn't think my negotiations were with you."

"But I think they should've been."

"Oh, yeah? What have you got to offer?"

"I thought you might consider a marriage of convenience?"

Jack stood there staring at Elizabeth, his face a blank slate. She couldn't read him.

After a moment he said, "Explain marriage of convenience."

"You know what it means, Jack! Don't act naive."

"So you're talking about a pretend marriage? And nothing else?"

"Right. We'd pretend to be— I mean, we'd be married legally, but we wouldn't—"

He cut her off with the wave of a hand. "Nope. I don't want to go the rest of my life without sex."

Elizabeth's hands flew to her cheeks. Underneath she felt heat building up. "But we couldn't— That would be too— We couldn't!"

"Why not? I'm attracted to you. Haven't you thought about maybe testing the waters?"

"No! Absolutely not!"

"Are you being honest?" he asked.

She stepped back slightly from him. "Yes, I'm being honest!"

"So now you know the difference between a man and a woman. Men frequently don't think of anything else."

"That can't be true."

"I'm afraid it is. And I wouldn't even consider a marriage without sex. Especially with you."

There went her cheeks again, flaring up. "Why would you say that?"

"Because I think you're sexy."

Her blue eyes opened wide and she stared at him.

"Now you look like Jenny." He moved a couple of steps closer to her. "Maybe I should kiss you. A good, long kiss this time just to see if we're compatible."

She backed up, but he pursued her, as if they were doing a dance. Before she knew it, he wrapped his arms tightly around her and took her lips in a blistering kiss.

It wasn't that she found his lips distasteful. Nor did she hate his arms wrapped tightly around her. It was that she didn't want to admit that she was attracted to him. If she admitted that, she had to admit the possibility of a real marriage.

He deepened the kiss, stirring her emotions.

Suddenly she pulled away from him and ran from the barn.

"Elizabeth!"

Jack's shout followed her, but she ignored it, running as if the hounds of hell were at her feet.

Thoughts of Elizabeth occupied Jack's mind the rest of the afternoon. He couldn't stop reliving their kiss in the barn.

He purposely hadn't run after her. When he approached her the next time, they needed to be alone, without any little ears listening.

Tonight he'd try to catch her alone, after Brady was in bed. Maybe after she'd fed Jenny.

He dug the spade into the feed, hard and deep, as if taking out his frustrations on it. He was not a virgin, but he also didn't spend his nights flirting with every single woman in town. His daddy had explained the way women were wired. They wanted a man to do the work while they made a nest. He'd done the work here with Tom, and it was ready for a woman to make it a home.

He wanted that woman to be Elizabeth.

With her, he could have a beautiful wife and two fine kids. He loved them already. Brady was a fine son, raised well by his mother. And Jenny was beautiful. And who knew? Maybe one day they'd add to their little family.

But he couldn't consider marrying

Elizabeth if he wasn't allowed to touch her. That would be impossible.

Elizabeth took a moment to compose herself before she went back into the house, the safe house where Jack wasn't allowed to touch her.

When she went in, she found her son waiting for her.

"Did you talk to Jack, Mommy?"

She hated to lie to her son, but she thought it was necessary in this instance. "No, I couldn't find him."

"'Cause I was thinking that maybe Jack would help me with a puppy. You know, teach me how to raise it. That would be neat, wouldn't it?"

"Yes, sweetheart, that would be neat, but I don't think Jack would have time to help you."

"Why not?" Brady asked.

"He…he has to raise the cows. They take a lot of work."

"Wouldn't he have time at night?"

"I…I don't know. I can't think about that right now."

"Did you ask him about being my daddy?"

"No! I told you I didn't talk to him."

"Oh. 'Cause I'd share him with Jenny."

"That's nice of you, Brady." She suddenly wondered where Carol was. "Where is Carol?"

"She's having a talk with Grandpa. I think they're kissing."

Elizabeth stared at her son. "Why do you say that?"

"'Cause Grandpa said he was sorry. And Grandma said she forgave him."

"You've had a very busy afternoon, haven't you, sweetie?"

"Yeah, but can't you go back out and look for Jack? I think he'd like to be my daddy."

"No! I don't think Jack would like that. Some men don't like little boys."

"Was Daddy like that?"

"No…yes, sweetheart, he was. And I didn't mean Jack doesn't like you, because he does. Mommy just got confused, that's all."

"I'm glad Jack likes me."

"Yes, sweetheart, Jack does like you. He just— It's too complicated to explain right now."

"Can we ask him at dinner?"

She could just hear Brady asking Jack why he didn't want to be his daddy. That was all she needed. "No, we don't ask personal questions at dinner."

"Why not?"

"Because it makes people feel uncomfortable. I'll talk to him another time." She heard Jenny's cry as she awakened. "I have to take care of Jenny right now."

"Okay, Mommy."

She ran up the stairs to Jenny's room, but her daughter was sound asleep. Sitting in the rocker, she planned to stay there anyway. At least Jenny wouldn't ask her any questions.

When Jack reached the house for dinner, his mind was occupied with Elizabeth. He wondered if she'd thought any more about their relationship. He certainly had. It seemed to him that he and Elizabeth were meant for each other.

When he came into the kitchen Carol was at the stove. Elizabeth wasn't anywhere in sight.

"Where's Elizabeth?"

Carol turned to stare at him. "Do you need her?"

"No, not really. I just wondered where she was."

"I believe she's helping Brady prepare his room in case Santa brings him a puppy."

"Ah, I see. I'll go up and see if I can help."

He double-timed his way to the second floor. He heard Elizabeth's voice in Brady's room. "What's this I hear about Santa maybe delivering a puppy to Jenny?" he teased.

"No! To me!" Brady screamed in excitement.

"To you? Are you sure you're big enough to have a puppy?"

"Yeah! I'm lots bigger than Jenny."

He loved Brady's smile. "I must've misunderstood. You're right, you're much bigger than Jenny."

"Do you think the puppy will like it here?" Brady asked, his eyes big with excitement.

"I think this will be the perfect room for a puppy. But you have to learn how to train a puppy so he'll be happy."

Brady turned to his mother. "Mommy, do you know how to train a puppy?"

"No, sweetheart, I don't." She sank her teeth into her bottom lip.

"I could teach both of you, but Brady, it requires a lot of work."

"I can learn, Jack. I'll work really hard."

"Is that all right with you, Elizabeth?" he asked, meeting her gaze for the first time.

Her voice cool, she turned away from him. "I don't know if you'll be here long enough. Maybe we should just wait, Brady, until we're more settled."

Jack knew Brady was on his side. He studied the proud woman for a minute.

"I think there will be enough time. After all, Santa's coming next week, isn't he?"

"Yeah! There's time, Mommy. I'll learn everything Jack says. I promise!"

"Count on it, Brady. You and I can work things out."

"Yippee! Jack, can I have the black puppy? With the white tip on his tail?"

"You know, I was thinking that would be the perfect dog for you."

"Jack, I love you!"

"Brady, you can't have a dog unless I approve!" Elizabeth said, but it had no effect on Brady. He was dancing around his room, singing and clapping.

Jack took Elizabeth's arm and drew her out of the room. "Stop trying to rain on his parade."

"That's easy for you to say. You'll be gone before the tears come."

"There won't be any tears if I get my way," Jack said. Then he leaned his head down and kissed her again.

She was so stunned by his kiss, she found herself kissing him back out of instinct.

Instinct? Or desire?

Before she could answer, Jack pulled back.

"Now that wasn't so bad, was it?" He smiled at her. "I think I like kissing you."

Before Elizabeth could lie and deny she

liked kissing Jack, Jenny let out an angry cry. "What's wrong with Jenny?" she questioned.

"I don't know. Is she supposed to be up at five o'clock?"

"No. I just put her down an hour ago," Elizabeth said as she rushed to Jenny's room.

Jack followed her. Elizabeth bent over her baby and recognized Jenny was very hot. "I think she's running a fever."

"Let me call Doc and see if he'll wait a few minutes until we can get her there."

Elizabeth gathered up the necessities to take the baby while Jack called the doctor. She asked Carol to watch Brady, then they hurried out the door, her sick baby clutched to her bosom.

CHAPTER TWELVE

WHEN Jack assisted a weary Elizabeth into his truck after the doctor saw Jenny, he instructed her to slide over to the center of the seat so he could belt Jenny's car seat into the far passenger seat. Now that the baby would be fine, he knew Elizabeth needed someone to lean on.

She proved he was right, because she did so without protesting.

When he rounded his truck and slid behind the wheel, Elizabeth was sitting next to him. Very next to him.

He started the engine. Then he wrapped his arm around Elizabeth. "This stuff really takes a toll on you, doesn't it?"

"Yes, it does." After a moment she added, "But it was nice to have someone to share the worry with this time."

"I can't imagine you going through this alone. Did you ever have an incident like this with Brady?"

"No," Elizabeth said with a sigh. "I didn't have anything urgent with Brady. I might've been more calm if I had."

"Well, it certainly was a first time for me." He looked over at Jenny. "Is she still doing all right?"

"Yes, she is. Her temperature seems lower and she's sleeping soundly. Amazing how innocent and peaceful she looks now."

They rode along in silence for a few minutes, Jack casting glances at Elizabeth and loving the feel of her thigh against his. When he stopped for a red light he bent down and kissed her forehead.

Rather than protest, Elizabeth laid her head down on his shoulder. She had one hand on Jenny, just to be sure, and her head on Jack's shoulder.

When they reached the house, Jack bent and kissed her lips before he got out to come around. Releasing Jenny's seat belt, he took the baby out and reached for Elizabeth.

She slid out of the truck and then hurried inside. The wind was still sharp and the warmth of the house was welcome.

Tom and Carol greeted them, questions about Jenny tumbling from their lips.

"She's fine," Jack reassured them. "The doctor said she's got an ear infection and her temperature just got out of hand. Doc gave her some antibiotics."

"That'll make her better," Carol reassured them.

"I have something even better than that," Elizabeth said with a laugh. "I have Jack to sing to her."

Tom laughed a belly laugh, then stifled it as he realized the baby was sleeping. "I didn't know you could sing, Jack," he teased his friend.

"I can manage enough to get Jenny's attention. She listens to me and goes to sleep."

"Is that because your singing is so bad?" Tom grinned.

Elizabeth came to his rescue. "I won't have you teasing Jack, Tom. He was invaluable while we were in the doctor's office."

"We're just glad Jenny's all right," Carol said. "We went ahead and ate, but I saved dinner for you two. I'll hold the baby while you eat."

When the meal was finished, Elizabeth got up to do the dishes. Jack joined her, loading the dishwasher.

"Thanks, Jack," Elizabeth whispered before she turned to take her baby. She'd fixed a bottle and took Jenny upstairs, cuddling her close to her. "Thanks for everything."

"No problem, Elizabeth," he called out to her.

He wished she knew how much it meant to him to be a valuable part of her family tonight.

Jack went into the den and settled down beside Brady to watch a little television. Brady leaned into Jack's arm and whispered, "I sure was glad Jenny was okay."

"Yeah, buddy, me, too."

"Is Mommy okay?"

"Yeah, she is. She was worried about Jenny, but since she's all right, so is your mommy."

"Good. Can Mommy come watch the Christmas show with us?"

"I don't think so. She'd got to keep an eye on your sister."

"Okay."

The show had a puppy in it, and Brady was almost beside himself, wanting to talk about the dog.

"I'm working on your mom. But you need to not ask her about your puppy."

"Okay, I promise."

When the show was over and Elizabeth still hadn't come down, Jack took Brady up to get his bath. "Have you ever taken a shower?" he asked the boy.

"What's a shower?"

"That's what most men take. Want to try one?"

"Will it be okay with Mommy?"

"Sure," Jack assured him.

When Elizabeth had settled Jenny down for the night, she thought about going down to take care of Brady, but she thought Brady would come up when the program was over. And she desperately needed some time to herself.

She went to her room and lay down on her bed. Just a few minutes was all she needed. While she shut her eyes, she was thinking about Jack. He'd been wonderful tonight. Considerate and protective. She'd never been treated so wonderfully.

The next thing she knew, Jack was awakening her.

"Honey, you need to put on your pajamas and get in bed."

She came awake immediately. "No, I need to bathe Brady and put him to bed."

"He's already in bed. Just go kiss him good-night."

"But he needed a bath."

"Yeah, but I gave him a shower. He's squeaky clean, I promise."

Elizabeth got up and headed for Brady's room. "Are you all right, sweetie?" she asked as she hugged him.

"Yeah, Mommy. Jack gave me a shower."

"Did you like it?" she asked.

"Yeah, Mommy, it's great!"

"All right. As long as you're clean. Give me a good-night kiss. Thank you. Now let's say your prayers."

Once Brady was settled, Elizabeth left his bedroom with Jack. In the hall, Jack took her in his arms. "I want you to know that tonight meant a lot to me."

"Jack—"

"Ssh, don't say anything." He bent down and kissed her.

Then he turned her around and nudged her toward her bedroom.

Elizabeth lay in her bed, unable to sleep. Thoughts of Jack raced through her head.

In the few weeks she'd known him, Jack

had shown her more love and consideration than Reggie had ever done. He'd also shown her children more love and protection.

She'd given Reggie five years of her life. What did she owe Jack? At least twice as much time. But could she leave him after that time? No, she didn't think she could leave him after whatever amount of time he spent with her.

She loved him.

There was no sense in denying it anymore. As much as she swore she'd never marry again, tomorrow she'd tell Jack that she could agree to a real marriage. If that was what he wanted. She didn't think it would be necessary to tell him she loved him. She didn't want to admit that.

Could she conduct such an agreement and keep her secret safe?

She hoped so.

* * *

Eager to see Elizabeth, Jack came running down the steps for breakfast the next morning. Was she going to retreat from him? He hoped not, not after last night.

He'd been up all night, going over in his mind how right it was to marry Elizabeth. He had to find a way to claim her and her children. They were right for him. And he was right for them.

When he didn't see Elizabeth in the kitchen, his heart fell. Then she stepped out from behind the pantry door, and he almost fell to his knees.

"Elizabeth, I thought you weren't down here."

She appeared to be surprised. "Why wouldn't I be down here?"

"I thought you might skip breakfast."

"Of course not."

"I'm glad." He smiled at her and was relieved to receive a smile in return.

He pulled out his seat and was served breakfast. He was just taking his last bite when Elizabeth said, "I'd like to talk to you again about…about your suggestion for the future when you have time."

Judging from the way she avoided his gaze, he figured it wasn't good news.

He wanted to shout at her, to tell her she couldn't manage without him. Instead he put down his fork and said, "I'm ready."

"You want to talk now?"

"Yeah, I do. I think I reserve the right to talk you into marrying me, even if that's not your decision today. I won't give up. I'm telling you that now."

"You won't?" Elizabeth said in surprise.

"No. We're going to be happy, Elizabeth. I promise you that." He punctuated his promise with his finger.

"All right."

He waved the finger at her. "I won't take— What did you say?"

"I said yes."

He almost turned over the table in his hurry to reach her. "You said yes?"

She nodded. "I said yes."

"Yes, you'll marry me?"

"Yes, definitely."

"A real marriage, not one of those imitation marriages."

"Yes."

He kissed her, long and tenderly, and then turned and headed for the stairs with Elizabeth in tow.

"Wait! Jack, what are you doing?"

"I want to take you to bed. I've been thinking about that for as long as you've been here. I don't want to wait any longer."

"Jack, you're going to have the rest of your life to make love to me. Don't you think that will be long enough?"

"Are you saying no for now?"

"Yes, the rest of the family will be up in a few minutes. It wouldn't be appropriate."

He had to admit she was right. "All right. And I suppose you want to wait until we're married?"

"It would be nice, but I don't think I'll be able to wait that long myself, unless we get married at Christmas."

"Done! I'll call the pastor this morning. He won't mind a small ceremony on Christmas Day."

She giggled as she heard Brady coming down the stairs.

"You'd better turn me loose unless you want to answer a lot of questions," Elizabeth teased.

"I don't mind the questions, because I got the right answer."

"Hi, Mommy, Jack. Why are you holding Mommy, Jack."

"Hi, Brady. I'm holding your mommy because she's just agreed to marry me."

"Really?" Brady asked before he had another question. "So Jack will be my daddy?"

"Yes, Brady," his mother said, "you get a new daddy for Christmas."

"Oh, boy! That's neat!"

"It also means you get a new puppy, because I'll be here to teach you how to train him," Jack said.

"Yippee! Santa is going to bring me everything I want!"

"You are one lucky little boy," Jack said as he turned loose of Elizabeth and picked up Brady and spun him around the room.

But not as lucky as he.

Elizabeth tried to stay organized the next few days, what with Christmas and the wedding to consider. She knew that Jack had accepted her agreement as a practical thing. And it was. But she knew in her heart that she loved him.

So why was she afraid to tell him?

Because she didn't want to be vulnerable.

Not again.

Brady was so excited about her marriage to Jack, that he was already calling him Daddy. Jenny would grow up calling him that too and not knowing any other father. She was a lucky little girl to have Jack as her daddy, rather than the real man who had fathered her.

As happy as she was for her children, she was just as happy for herself.

Jack comforted her. He opened his arms for her to lean into. He made her laugh.

He restored her faith in love.

Then why not tell him how she felt about him?

Finally she made up her mind. She had to be

honest with him before he committed to marrying her.

The night before Christmas, after she'd put some gifts under the tree, she asked Jack about the puppy. "Will you bring in the puppy in the morning before Brady comes down?"

"Yeah, we don't want to leave an adventurous puppy here all night."

"Okay. I've prepared a box with holes so he can breathe. It's right here. You can just put him inside and put the lid on top."

"That's great, honey. He's going to be so excited."

"Yes, he is." She paused before she said, "Are we doing the right thing, Jack?"

He gave her a sharp look. "You mean about the marriage?"

She nodded.

He put down some presents he was adding

to the pile under the tree and turned to look at her. "Are you having second thoughts?"

"I just want to be sure that we're doing the right thing."

He took her in his arms. "Yes, Elizabeth, we're doing the right thing."

"How do you know?"

"I know that you don't love me, Elizabeth, but I'll be good to you. We can provide your two kids some stability, a two-parent marriage and a good home. Isn't that important?"

"Yes, of course it is. But what are you getting out of this?" She pulled back, her eyes searching his face.

"I get to make love to you. That is part of the deal, isn't it?"

"Yes, but what if I'm terrible at it? I couldn't keep Reggie interested enough. What if you don't even like making love to me?"

"I think I can take that risk." He grinned at her but she wasn't sure.

Finally, he said, "Look, honey, I'll be willing to make love to you as long as you're willing to let me. I haven't told you I love you. But I do. So—"

"You love me?" she asked, stunned by his words. Suddenly she broke into a smile. "Jack, I love you, too!"

He stared at her. "I don't believe you."

"I didn't want to tell you because I was afraid it'd make me vulnerable again. But now that you've confessed, I can, too."

He pulled her into his arms and kissed her, and Elizabeth knew Jack was right. They were meant to be.

"We could go upstairs and anticipate our wedding vows," he said with a devilish gleam in his eye. "Are you interested?"

"Yes, I'm interested, but I don't think we

should do that. I don't want to have Brady find us in bed together before the magic words are spoken."

"I guess you're right. But I wanted to make love to you for a long time."

"Brady wouldn't understand," she told him.

"No, I guess he wouldn't. And he's going to have enough presents to open in the morning. I guess he doesn't need one to shock him."

She leaned against him and kissed him.

After returning her kiss with great enthusiasm, Jack said, "I think you're right. But after tonight he'll have to get used to finding you in my bed, because that's where you're going to be."

"You won't hear any complaints from me."

0309 Rom LP

MILLS & BOON PUBLISH EIGHT LARGE PRINT TITLES A MONTH. THESE ARE THE EIGHT TITLES FOR APRIL 2009.

———————— ✿ ————————

THE GREEK TYCOON'S DISOBEDIENT BRIDE
Lynne Graham

THE VENETIAN'S MIDNIGHT MISTRESS
Carole Mortimer

RUTHLESS TYCOON, INNOCENT WIFE
Helen Brooks

THE SHEIKH'S WAYWARD WIFE
Sandra Marton

THE ITALIAN'S CHRISTMAS MIRACLE
Lucy Gordon

CINDERELLA AND THE COWBOY
Judy Christenberry

HIS MISTLETOE BRIDE
Cara Colter

PREGNANT: FATHER WANTED
Claire Baxter

MILLS & BOON
Pure reading pleasure

MILLS & BOON PUBLISH EIGHT LARGE PRINT TITLES A MONTH. THESE ARE THE EIGHT TITLES FOR MAY 2009.

— ◌ℛ —

THE BILLIONAIRE'S BRIDE OF VENGEANCE
Miranda Lee

THE SANTANGELI MARRIAGE
Sara Craven

THE SPANIARD'S VIRGIN HOUSEKEEPER
Diana Hamilton

THE GREEK TYCOON'S RELUCTANT BRIDE
Kate Hewitt

NANNY TO THE BILLIONAIRE'S SON
Barbara McMahon

CINDERELLA AND THE SHEIKH
Natasha Oakley

PROMOTED: SECRETARY TO BRIDE!
Jennie Adams

THE BLACK SHEEP'S PROPOSAL
Patricia Thayer

MILLS & BOON
Pure reading pleasure